"Let's do it," Mimi said

Seth jumped. "Do it?"

"Yeah, let's go." Mimi hiked up her dress, revealing those beautiful legs of hers, and got out of the car.

Seth jerked his brain back to reality. She meant for them to take the last room, not do *it*. They were complete opposites. He didn't want Mimi to be attracted to him.

Even if she was the sexiest woman he'd ever laid eyes on.

He locked the car and followed her, determined to keep his thoughts on track. He reminded himself that he'd felt sorry for Mimi earlier, and had planned to offer her a shoulder to cry on if she were still upset.

So they'd share a room later as friends—no, *acquaintances.* It was no big deal. No one would ever know they'd been stranded together. It was only for one night.

What could possibly go wrong?

Dear Reader,

Spring is the perfect time to celebrate the joy of romance. So get set to fall in love as Harlequin American Romance brings you four new spectacular books.

First, we're happy to welcome *New York Times* bestselling author Kasey Michaels to the Harlequin American Romance family. She inaugurates TEXAS SHEIKHS, our newest in-line continuity, with *His Innocent Temptress*. This four-book series focuses on a Texas family with royal Arabian blood who must fight to reunite their family and reclaim their rightful throne.

Also, available this month, *The Virgin Bride Said, "Wow!"* by Cathy Gillen Thacker, a delightful marriage-of-convenience story and the latest installment in THE LOCKHARTS OF TEXAS miniseries. Kara Lennox provides fireworks as a beautiful young woman who's looking for Mr. Right sets out to *Tame an Older Man* following the advice of 2001 WAYS TO WED, a book guaranteed to provide satisfaction! And *Have Baby, Need Beau* says it all in Rita Herron's continuation of her wonderful THE HARTWELL HOPE CHESTS series.

Enjoy April's selections and come back next month for more love stories filled with heart, home and happiness from Harlequin American Romance.

Wishing you happy reading,

Melissa Jeglinski
Associate Senior Editor
Harlequin American Romance

HAVE BABY, NEED BEAU

Rita Herron

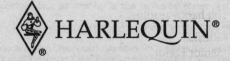

HARLEQUIN®

TORONTO • NEW YORK • LONDON
AMSTERDAM • PARIS • SYDNEY • HAMBURG
STOCKHOLM • ATHENS • TOKYO • MILAN • MADRID
PRAGUE • WARSAW • BUDAPEST • AUCKLAND

To Karen Solem for loving this idea as much as I did!

ISBN 0-373-16872-1

HAVE BABY, NEED BEAU

ABOUT THE AUTHOR

Rita Herron is a teacher, workshop leader and storyteller who loves reading, writing and sharing stories with people of all ages. She has published two nonfiction books for adults on working and playing with children, and has won the Golden Heart award for a young adult story. Rita believes that books taught her to dream, and she loves nothing better than sharing that magic with others. She lives with her "dream" husband and three children, two cats and a dog in Norcross, Georgia.

Books by Rita Herron

HARLEQUIN AMERICAN ROMANCE

820—HIS-AND-HERS TWINS
859—HAVE GOWN, NEED GROOM*
872—HAVE BABY, NEED BEAU*

*The Hartwell Hope Chests

HARLEQUIN INTRIGUE

486—SEND ME A HERO
523—HER EYEWITNESS
556—FORGOTTEN LULLABY
601—SAVING HIS SON

My spunky little Mimi,

You have always been special to me because you were the middle child, the one who tagged along to her older sister's recitals, the one who wore hand-me-downs and rolled with the punches whenever there were problems. You never ran from a fight, never fussed when your dad was too busy working to come home at night, never complained that you never got anything first. You have a heart of gold, an infectious smile and a soft spot for strays. You made us laugh when we thought there might never be laughter in the house again.

You are feisty and witty, creative and determined, but independent to a fault. You know how to have fun in life and laugh at your problems. You are a survivor. I hope you learn to trust in others, to take comfort, as well as offer it.

I wish for you happiness and true love, and a man who will be your equal and give you all the joy a partner can give.

Love you always,

Grammy Rose

Chapter One

"I can't believe Hannah is actually married." Mimi Hartwell gazed at the beautiful white ribbons and roses adorning the gazebo, drawing her finger across her neck in a slashing gesture. "Thank God it's not me."

Mimi's younger sister, Alison, elbowed her in the side and laughed. "Mimi, you're terrible! Hannah's happier than I've ever seen her."

"Yeah, but wait till the honeymoon's over."

Alison sighed dreamily. "The way the two of them were looking at each other during the ceremony, I think the honeymoon's going to last a long time."

Their father, Wiley, strutted forward and waved his arms like an air-traffic controller, his ruffled pink shirt and white shoes gleaming in the fading daylight, his chest puffed up with pride like a peacock. "All you single girls line up. It's time for Hannah to throw the bouquet."

Mimi blinked back tears at the joyous expression on her older sister's face when Hannah crested the top of the hill, still wearing her grandmother's wedding gown. In spite of the January temperature, which had steadily dropped all day, Hannah and Jake had pledged their vows earlier at her grandmother's property on top of Pine Mountain. Wiley had actually toned down his usual outlandish penchant for publicity stunts and allowed Hannah a serene wedding, but the girls' mother, whom they hadn't seen in a decade, had surprised them with her sudden appearance. Hannah had been distant toward her, Alison nonchalant, and Mimi had simply tried to joke about her appearance—all of them ignoring the stab of pain they felt seeing her now after so many lost years. Mimi scanned the crowd to see if she'd joined the bouquet catchers, but didn't spot her meticulously put-together mother anywhere.

A few nurses and doctors who worked with Hannah gathered to form a line. Even Grammy Rose jumped to the front and waved her bony hands as if she wanted to catch the cluster of red roses.

Alison jerked her arm. "Come on, Mimi. We have to get up front."

Mimi dug her rose-colored heels into the grass, determined to steer clear of the superstitious wedding nonsense. "I'm not participating."

"Look, I know you're allergic to roses, but—"

"It's not my allergy. But I'm never getting married, so there's no reason to fight for the bouquet."

"Listen, Mimi, just because Joey was arrested doesn't mean you won't find someone else. Someone better than him."

Mimi winced at the reminder of her boyfriend, her *ex*-boyfriend, she amended silently. Boy, she sure could pick 'em. Not only had she failed at this relationship thing, but she'd let her father down by dating a man who'd been stealing from him. Not that Wiley blamed her—

"Hurry up, ladies." Wiley slapped his new son-in-law on the back. "The groom's impatient to leave."

Jake curved his brawny arm around Hannah, and a sheepish grin lit his face. "The weatherman's predicting a snowstorm. We need to leave before the roads ice over."

The guests laughed, not fooled at all by his statement.

"Come on." Alison yanked Mimi's arm again. "You know Hannah will throw the bouquet to one of us."

Mimi held firm, laughing at Alison's impatience. "Go on. Maybe you'll be the next Hartwell to take the plunge."

Alison frowned, but finally gave up and raced to the line just as Hannah tossed the arrangement over her shoulder. Shouts rang out across the lawn, laughter and squeals comingling. Mimi glanced sideways to see Seth, Hannah's ex-fiancé, standing under Grammy's big magnolia tree, his hands in his pockets, his expression slightly lost. She knew exactly how he felt. They had both been unlucky in love lately. Was Seth still hurting over Hannah?

Poor guy. If he wasn't quite so uptight and knew how to have fun, she or Alison might be attracted to him. The man was definitely handsome, but... What was she thinking?

Even if he *was* incredibly handsome, the three sisters had an unspoken rule about not dating one another's boyfriends. Ex-boyfriends included. Besides, Seth Broadhurst had been at her apartment when Joey's arrest aired on TV—they had watched the horrid scene together. So humiliating.

The women squealed and jostled one another in a good-natured attempt to catch the hurled bouquet. Mimi's eyes widened as the thing sailed over their heads and soared straight toward her. Her first instinct was to run. But she didn't have time—she reached out and yelped just before the bouquet smacked her in the face.

SETH BROADHURST laughed at the stunned expression on Mimi's face as she clutched the bouquet. Mimi sneezed, then spun toward the women congratulating her on her luck. Looking panic-stricken, she tried to stuff the bouquet in Alison's hands as if it was a live snake, rather than a cluster of beautiful roses. But Alison laughed and teased her, chanting, "Mimi's getting married, Mimi's getting married," while the other women clapped. Wiley's camera crew snapped pictures, capturing the moment to add to the litany of Hartwell news that had recently hit the papers.

Seth almost felt sorry for Mimi.

She looked ill at ease. Her ex-boyfriend's recent arrest and the subsequent speculation about her possible criminal involvement had obviously affected her.

Wiley had defended his daughter to the end. Ever the entrepreneur, he'd turned the tables and used the publicity to his advantage in his used-car business. But Hannah's new love, now Mimi's brother-in-law, was the cop who'd arrested Joey, so the situation had to be awkward for Mimi. She and Seth hadn't been close when he'd dated Hannah, but he sensed an innocence in Mimi that brought out his protective instincts. Although Mimi was impulsive, slightly scatterbrained and not quite as reliable as Hannah, he admired their closeness and would have hated to see a rift between the sisters.

As a psychiatrist, he should try to help Mimi.

Of course, becoming her therapist might pose a conflict of interest for him.

A strong breeze stirred the pine trees, and thick snowflakes began to fall, the whistle of the wind signaling the onset of the winter storm that had been predicted for the north-Georgia mountains. The guests suddenly dispersed, congratulations and hugs floating through the crowd as they hurried to leave. Seth spotted Trudy, one of the young physician's assistants from the hospital heading in his direction. From the glint in her eye, the wedding had given her ideas of snagging her own man. Hoping to avoid being the target of her manhunt, he slid in among the crowd as they congregated to toss birdseed on the departing newlyweds. He'd try to catch a word with Mimi before he headed back to town. Then he'd be out of the Hartwell family's lives for good.

Mimi stashed the bouquet in her grandmother's refrigerator next to Grammy's homemade muscadine wine, with a note asking her to preserve the arrangement for Hannah. This wedding hoopla made her nervous.

"Mimi, honey." Grammy Rose's thick, sturdy

heels clicked on the hardwood floor intermittently with her hand-painted cane. "I was looking for you. I have something to give you before you leave."

Mimi closed the refrigerator door, expecting an assortment of handmade crocheted pot holders or some of her grandmother's famous peach preserves, but instead, Grammy Rose grabbed her hand and dragged her to the parlor. Mimi was assaulted by memories at the sight of the antiques and family photos on the wall. Grammy pointed to a large, gold-embossed chest similar to the one she'd sent Hannah—the chest that had turned Hannah's life upside down. Mimi's stomach quivered.

"I have your hope chest ready, sweetheart. I want you to take it home today."

Mimi gulped. First all the wedding hoopla. Then the bouquet. Now her hope chest. "But, Grammy, I...I'm not getting married."

"Pshaw." Her grandmother raised gnarled fingers to brush a strand of gray hair back into her bun. "Of course you'll get married one day, dear."

"No, I mean I'm *never* getting married."

"Don't be silly." Her grandmother laughed. "You caught the bouquet today. You're next in line."

Mimi shook her head. "I'm not even dating anyone. And I just broke up with my boyfriend."

"Why, honey, I knew that Joey boy was just a passing fancy. The right man will come along, you mark my words."

"But I'm not looking for a husband, Grammy."

Grammy completely ignored her protests. "You

want me to get Wiley to help you put the chest in your car?''

''But, Grammy—''

''Or maybe we can carry it ourselves. We're modern women, right?'' Her grandmother bent to lift the chest, and Mimi imagined her precious grandmother's fragile bones cracking and popping through her skin any minute.

She panicked and waved her away with a gentle hand. ''No, Grammy. I'll get Dad or Alison to help me.''

''All right.'' Grammy Rose's eyes twinkled in triumph. ''I think Wiley wanted to leave right away on account of the storm,'' Grammy continued. ''Your mother already left.''

Mimi tried not to let that revelation upset her. Her mother hadn't even said goodbye. Of course, what had she expected? A joyous reunion as if her mother hadn't deserted them years ago? ''Alison and I should get on the road, too.''

Alison strolled in, nibbling on a finger-size eclair. Mimi's mouth fell open when she saw Seth Broadhurst behind her, looking like a lost puppy.

''Mimi, Dad's car won't start so he's going to ride with us in the Jeep.''

Giddy laughter bubbled up inside Mimi. How ironic. A used-car salesman with a car that wouldn't start.

She stared from her grandmother to her sister to Seth. Alison had just given her the perfect excuse. ''Sure. Grammy, I'll have to take the chest some other time.''

"Oh, honey, I did want you take it with you to-day." Grammy clutched a hand to her chest as if she might be having the big one. Mimi had seen her grandmother fake the gesture so many times she almost laughed.

"But there's no way we can fit all three of us and the chest in Alison's Jeep," Mimi said gently.

"I can give you a ride," Seth offered.

All eyes swung to him. He leaned against the door-jamb, a Val Kilmer look-alike with his warm brown eyes and sandy-colored hair. His whole demeanor seemed steeped in sexuality, something she'd never noticed before. "I have my Lexus. There's plenty of room in the trunk," Seth said in a low voice.

Mimi stammered a refusal, uncomfortable with the idea of Seth and the hope chest being in close proximity of each other. Odd things had happened after Hannah had opened *her* hope chest.

"Thanks, Seth," Alison said, answering for her. "Dad's in a hurry." Alison hugged her grandmother and strolled from the room, leaving Mimi with no choice but to accept the ride and take the hope chest with her.

But what the heck. Seth sounded so forlorn. He might be depressed about Hannah's marriage. Maybe he needed some company. She'd cheer him up just like she did when she took in a stray dog.

"So, WHY DIDN'T YOU WANT to take the chest with you?" Seth asked as he hoisted the bulky wooden box.

Mimi caught the opposite end, the two of them

shifting and juggling it sideways to fit through the front door. "What makes you think I didn't want to take it?"

"The look on your face," Seth said. "What gives?"

"It's tradition for the grandmother of the Hartwells to give each granddaughter a hope chest when she's getting married."

"You're getting married?" Seth asked.

Mimi shrugged at his incredulous tone. "No, never—the very reason I don't see the need for a hope chest."

"So you've sworn off men because of that creep Joey?"

"No, just commitment. I want a guy to have fun with."

And he wanted a woman to settle down with. They were complete opposites. Not that it mattered.

Still, somehow she looked vulnerable....

Mimi wobbled and accidentally slammed the chest into his side. He gritted his teeth to hide the pain shooting through his ribs. "Just angle it a little more to the right and I think we'll have it."

"Sorry," Mimi said softly.

Vulnerable, hell. She was a walking danger zone. Especially with that throaty voice.

Mimi caught her bottom lip with her teeth as she tried to follow his instructions, at the same time not letting the wooden doorjamb scrape the delicate gold embossing. For someone who didn't even want the chest, she certainly seemed determined to keep it from harm.

"Watch out for ice on the steps," Grammy warned. "That sky's so dark it reminds me of 'eighty-two when that blizzard knocked out everyone's power for days."

"I hope you'll be all right here, Grammy." Mimi looked worried. "Do you want to come to Sugar Hill with us?"

"Heavens, no," Grammy said. "I've got plenty of wood and canned food here to last me. And my buddy Winnie will be by directly to spend the night."

Seth's foot hit the slick wood and he wobbled, throwing Mimi off balance. She stumbled forward, almost taking out Seth's eye with the corner of the chest. He exhaled, thinking he'd be black-and-blue all over before they finished. Finally they both steadied themselves. He inched his feet along so he wouldn't fall as they descended the remaining steps and crossed the front yard.

Mimi's grandmother was right. The sky was black, the snow falling so thickly the dirt road was already blanketed. With the sun fading and the temperature dropping, the roads would ice over, making driving dangerous until the few snowplows available could be resurrected to clear the streets.

"There's Winnie now." Mimi's grandmother waved at an elderly lady in hot-pink sweats exiting a blue sedan. Seth wanted to offer his assistance, but he had his hands full. Instead, he nodded a greeting and veered sideways, leading Mimi down the dirt road toward his car. Mimi's grandmother yelled good-bye and ushered her friend inside. Snow crystals dotted Mimi's curly auburn hair and clung to her eyelashes. She must be freezing in that slinky rose-colored bridesmaid dress. Her breasts were practically spilling out, her nipples puckering against the satiny fabric.

"Where the heck did you park? Sugar Hill?" Mimi asked.

"No, but I arrived late, so I had to park down the hill."

"You could have moved your car up to the house," Mimi said.

Seth winced as his foot hit a rock. "You seemed in a rush to leave, but if you want to set this thing down, I'll go get it."

"It's not that heavy," Mimi said. "And I'd hate for the chest to get wet."

"You're awfully protective of something you don't want."

Mimi frowned at him as if he was a moron. "My grandmother did have it specially made for me. Don't you have any respect for family tradition?"

So, she had a sappy side to her, just as he'd suspected. Mimi was much more emotional than Hannah had ever been—that is, until the day Hannah had canceled their wedding. "My family isn't the sentimental type. What's in here, anyway?"

"I don't know. If it's like Hannah's, it's Pandora's box."

"What do you mean?"

"When Hannah opened her hope chest the night before her…er, your wedding, her whole life went crazy." Mimi blew her bangs from her eyes and averted her gaze.

"You mean her hope chest had something to do with that weird dream, the reason she canceled the wedding?"

"The ring was in her hope chest. It had that silly legend to it…"

They both eyed the gold chest with distrust.

"Look, Mimi, we still have a ways to go down the hill. Let's set it down and I'll go get the car." He blinked snow from his eyelashes and stumbled. His foot caught on a raised tree root and he lost his balance. He slid, yelping and trying to gain control.

His feet flew out from under him and the hope chest crashed down on his legs. Mimi toppled, too, landing on her stomach across the hope chest. Her arms cycled out by her sides as she struggled not to dive into the snow, and one fist smacked his eye. She rolled away and plopped into the cushiony snow beside him, anyway, and the latch to the chest suddenly sprang open.

It took them both a moment to realize what had happened. Seth pushed the chest aside to the ground. Mimi jumped up, shivering from the cold. The snow had dampened her dress, causing the silky material to cling to her voluptuous body. The damp bodice accentuated the fullness of her breasts, and the neckline dipped precariously off her shoulder, giving him a glimpse of luscious cleavage and creamy skin.

He stood and slapped the snow off his suit, dragging his gaze from her tempting body. He absolutely could not allow himself to be attracted to Mimi Hartwell. She was his ex-fiancée's sister, for heaven's sake. Plus, she was definitely the wrong type of woman for him. Mimi stared at him, and he noticed that the corner of the chest had ripped a hole in the crotch of his pants. He plastered his hands over his nearly visible privates and froze.

They both jerked their eyes from each other and spoke at the same time. "I'll go get the car."

"Go get the car."

He clutched the front of his pants together with his hands and hauled himself down the hill, praying Mimi hadn't noticed his burgeoning arousal.

MIMI GAPED AT SETH'S departing back, shocked to see he'd been turned on by her klutzy moves. The man must miss Hannah terribly *and* be completely desperate. Of course, he was a man, and his physical reaction had probably been simply that, a male reaction, not real attraction, or the man wouldn't be running down the icy drive as if a hungry lion was chomping at his heels.

She shivered. Her feet were wet and starting to get cold inside the dress shoes. The top of the chest stood open, the contents fairly begging to be examined. Curiosity won over her fear of superstition, and she peeked inside. Hannah's life had gone berserk the day she'd opened her hope chest.

What in the world had her grandmother put inside hers?

Chapter Two

Had Grammy Rose also given her an heirloom ring to wear so she would dream about her future husband?

Impossible. She was never getting married.

Mimi laughed and ran her finger over the hope chest's velvety grape-colored lining. On top of the lavender tissue paper lay a pale pink envelope, but she heard Seth's car coming, so she stuffed the letter in her purse, deciding to read it as they drove.

Seth parked the Lexus and climbed out, snow dotting his thick hair and glistening on his bronzed skin. He'd buttoned his suit coat to hide the tear in his pants. Mimi stifled a giggle.

"What's inside?" Seth asked.

"I'm afraid to look."

"Don't be silly. Nothing in there could possibly affect your future."

Mimi bit down on her lip. Seth lifted the tissue paper and her stomach flip-flopped. A beautiful bouquet lay in the center of the hope chest.

Two wedding bouquets in one day—not a good sign.

"Grammy Rose carried this bouquet when she married Gramps. I saw a picture of it in her photo album."

"See, nothing so strange about that."

Right. Nothing earth-shattering happened. No knight in shining armor appeared. Just dull Seth Broadhurst in a gray Lexus.

Mimi pushed aside the remaining tissue, her gaze resting on a blue-and-white baby quilt, a rocking-horse design appliquéed on the front. An antique silver baby rattle lay beside it.

"Now I *know* Grammy's confused," Mimi said with a nervous giggle. "I'm certainly not mommy material."

"Anyone can see that."

Mimi narrowed her eyes. "What does *that* mean?"

"Nothing." Seth shifted onto his other foot. "Just that I can't see you having kids."

"Well, I can't see you having them, either."

Seth arched a brow. "And why is that?"

"You'd probably psychoanalyze them to death."

"I would not."

"So you want children?" Mimi asked.

"That's not what I meant."

"Then what did you mean?"

"Forget it." Seth glanced up at the dark clouds. "Hurry up and see what else is in there so we can get going."

Mimi nodded, still stinging from his comment about her and motherhood. "Look, Grammy included her recipe book."

"I guess she thought you could use it at the coffee shop."

"I'm not going to work there forever," Mimi said, slightly defensive. "I'm trying out for a part in that soap opera that's going to be filmed in Atlanta called *Scandalous*. They need a belly dancer." Mimi turned around and shook her body, snowflakes splashing her cheeks.

THE IMAGE OF Mimi Hartwell in a harem costume was sexy and titillating. Not at all an appropriate way for Seth to be thinking about Hannah's sister.

He quickly squelched it. Mimi was a bona fide wannabe actress who probably changed boyfriends more often than he changed socks. Besides, the storm was getting worse and they needed to move.

Mimi slammed the chest shut. "Let's put it in the car and get going."

Grateful to be pulled back into reality, Seth helped her lift the hope chest and situate it in his trunk. Mimi rushed to the passenger side and climbed in, shivering and damp. He jumped in and turned on the heater, wishing he'd invested in snow tires.

Mimi adjusted the radio to a soft-rock station and began to hum softly, her voice melodious and rich, her hands fidgeting with an envelope in her hand. He turned his attention to his driving, the wind swirling snow through the wooded area around them, the road already growing slick. Tree limbs bowed with the weight of the snow, and a bitter wind wheezed through the trees, occasionally cracking thin branches and flinging them into the road. He dodged the branches and braked, shifting to low gear as he wound down the mountain.

"This weather's making me nervous," Mimi finally said. "I can hardly see the road."

Seth was uneasy, too. "Now that it's dark, it's only going to get worse."

"You think we'll make it back to Sugar Hill?"

Seth shrugged, his shoulders tight as he gripped the steering wheel. "I'll do my best to get us there."

The envelope rustled in Mimi's hands as she twisted them together. "Good, I have plans later on tonight."

A date? Had Mimi already recovered from Joey and moved on to someone else? Or was she planning to visit Joey in prison?

The thought irked him, although he didn't know why.

The car was growing warm, and he saw that she'd relaxed, so he adjusted the heat, faintly aware of the exotic scent of her perfume. With the windshield fogged, the blizzard whirling around them and some mellow oldie playing on the radio, the interior of the car suddenly seemed way too intimate.

He yanked at his tie, loosening the knot at his neck. "What *is* that perfume you're wearing?"

Mimi smiled, obviously thinking he liked the strong scent. "Passion Point. You're supposed to dab it on your..."

He arched a brow.

"Well, you know. All your erogenous zones."

Which must have been her whole body.

Seth swung his gaze back to the road, the blur of

imagined fantasies nearly blinding him to the white haze in front of him.

The radio announcer bleeped in. "Folks, we're in the midst of a full-fledged winter storm alert. Already some major expressways have been closed for safety reasons. We're advising you to stay off them. If you're a traveler, seek shelter in a hotel until morning when snowplows can clear the roads." He finished by listing areas suffering from downed power lines and trees.

"I guess we'd better try to find a hotel," he said.

Mimi narrowed her eyes as if spending the night at the same hotel with him was a horrendous imposition.

Well, he wasn't too happy about it, either, but he was too much of a gentlemen to say so. After all, he had an important date tonight, too.

Of course, his date was a copy of *Strategies for Coping with Divorce in the Single-Family Home,* but he didn't have to tell her that.

Mimi avoided looking at Seth, uneasy about the hazardous conditions, but Hannah had always claimed Seth was completely reliable. Not mind-boggling in the love department, but dependable. Come to think of it, Hannah had never mentioned that she'd slept with Seth, but Mimi had assumed they had. She'd also assumed Hannah hadn't talked about their love life because it had been lacking in umph. Seth probably had to consult his pocket calendar to schedule sex. Seth never did anything impetuous, could be depended on to keep a cool head—exactly what she needed when surrounded by a raging blizzard. Someone who wasn't driven by hormones, as Joey had been.

Feeling calmer, she opened the letter and smiled at her Grammy's loopy handwriting. She could almost hear her grandmother's Southern drawl...

My spunky little Mimi,
You have always been special to me because you were the middle child, the one who tagged along to her older sister's recitals, the one who wore hand-me-downs and rolled with the punches whenever there were problems. You never ran from a fight, never fussed when your dad was too busy working to come home at night, never complained that you never got anything first. You have a heart of gold, an infectious smile, and you're a sucker for strays. You made us laugh when we thought there might never be laughter in the house again.

You're feisty and witty, creative and determined, but independent to a fault. You know how to have fun in life and laugh at your problems. You are a survivor. I hope you learn to trust in others, to take comfort, as well as offer it.

I wish for you happiness and true love, and a man who will be your equal and give you all the joy a partner can give.

Love you always,
Grammy Rose

Mimi blinked back tears, her heart contracting. She'd always been the misfit child, the one who got in trouble. Hannah had been the responsible, studious one, the one everyone admired.

"What's wrong?" Seth asked.

Perceptive shrink, wasn't he? "Nothing," Mimi said, unable to voice how much the letter meant to her.

"Then why are you crying?"

"I'm not."

Seth shook his head as if irritated. "Why do women always do that?"

"Do what?"

"Get angry or upset, then claim nothing's wrong when a guy expresses concern."

"Maybe because it's none of your business."

Seth's mouth tightened. "Sorry. I was only trying to be nice."

"Or trying to analyze me, sneaky shrink-style."

He shot her a dark look. "I'm not a sneaky anything. Why are you so paranoid about psychiatrists, anyway?"

"There you go analyzing again. Must be a habit."

"I'm not analyzing you, Mimi. Like I said, I was only trying to be your friend."

Mimi shrugged. "Sorry. I guess I took it the wrong way. Must be that whole Mars-Venus thing."

"I guess." A small smile tugged at Seth's mouth. "There's a hotel over there. I'm going to stop."

"I'll wait in the car." Mimi gestured toward her bridesmaid's dress.

"Right. It might look a little odd."

Several cars filled the lot as Mimi toyed with the letter, rereading the heartfelt words while she waited.

Seth returned with a scowl on his face. "No rooms."

Mimi patted his arm. "Don't worry, Seth, we'll find something."

His blue eyes flickered with doubt, but Mimi believed in the value of optimism. He continued down the winding mountain. She searched for a music station on the radio, but every station focused on the weather, only adding to the mounting tension.

Thirty minutes later, Mimi's optimism had faded along with the visibility and any hope the blizzard would let up. Seth had tried a small motor lodge, a bed-and-breakfast and one place with a purple door and orange lights that Mimi had negated on sight—it looked a little seedy and was in a bad section of town. Finally they veered toward the apple houses near Ellijay. Seth clenched his jaw so tight she expected to hear bone grinding any minute. A few miles later, Mimi spotted a large well-known hotel, the Magnolia Manor.

"There have to be rooms here," she said, pointing to the long drive.

"Let's hope. I'm low on gas now and the highway's closed." Seth steered the car up the drive at a turtle's pace and parked in front of the sprawling hotel. He returned minutes later with a tight expression on his face.

"Don't tell me this big place doesn't have any rooms."

He held up his index finger. "No, they have one."

"That's great."

"Just one."

"What?"

"Just one room, as in a *single* one."

Mimi's stomach sank as Seth's meaning hit her. They would have to share.

SETH KNEW HE SHOULD offer to sleep in the car and let Mimi have the room to herself, but the idea of spending the night in the frigid temperatures was not appealing.

Mimi's face registered surprise, then indecision, and for a moment, worry. "Look, Mimi, I can sleep on the floor if you want. You know Hannah and I were... What I'm trying to say here is...er—"

"I know you're safe," Mimi said matter-of-factly. "Believe me, Seth, I'm not worried."

Seth bristled, wondering why she thought he was safe.

"I hope the bar's open. Maybe we can get a drink and relax. You must be stiff from driving."

"Um, yeah. I saw a bar in the lobby." His shoulders *were* aching from the tense maneuvers down the mountain. And Mimi's perfume had made him slightly dizzy. And *stiff.*

"I hope there's a gift shop, too. I need a toothbrush and something to sleep in. I have to get out of this silly bridesmaid dress."

Seth stifled the images her comment brought to mind. Helping Mimi out of the dress and her sleeping in his arms...ridiculous. He didn't even like her. Did he?

"Let's do it," Mimi said.

He nearly jumped out of his shoes. "Do it?"

"Yeah, let's go." She hiked up her dress, revealing those beautiful legs of hers, and yanked at the neck of the dress, which had slipped lower as the evening had worn on.

He jerked his brain back to reality. She meant for them to take the room, not do *it*. Obviously Mimi didn't find him attractive, another stomp on his wounded ego.

She preferred rough types like that jailbird ex-boyfriend of hers, guys with tattoos who probably drove motorcycles and had ungodly piercing of assorted body parts—the exact opposite of him.

Which was perfect. He didn't want Mimi to be attracted to him. Even if she was the sexiest woman he'd ever laid eyes on. She wanted to be a belly dancer, for God's sake. And he was a respected psychiatrist. She probably needed to lie on his couch and let him analyze her erratic behavior.

Not lie on his couch and have him analyze her in the physical sense.

He locked the car and followed her, grateful to see the open bar and determined to steer his thoughts back on track. He'd simply reacted to Mimi's comment. First Hannah had dumped him, then her sister had insulted his male prowess. And Mimi's exotic perfume, which had driven him crazy for the past half hour, probably had some chemical in it that had affected his brain cells. It was a wonder the pheromones hadn't asphyxiated him.

Reminding himself he'd felt sorry for Mimi earlier,

that he'd planned to offer her a shoulder to lean on if she was still upset over her boyfriend's deception, he straightened his tie and followed her. Yep, he'd put on his counseling hat and consider the evening with her as a job.

So they'd share a room later as friends—no, *acquaintances*—it was no big deal. No one but the two of them would ever know they'd been stranded together. And it was for *only* one night.

What could possibly go wrong?

Chapter Three

Mimi studied the frown on Seth's face as they settled on stools in the crowded bar. Was he pining for Hannah? Thinking about their lost wedding night? Wishing he was in the honeymoon suite with Hannah, instead of here with her?

Stupid question. Of course he did.

"What would you like?" Seth asked.

"Huh?"

"To drink?"

Mimi noticed the bartender watching her, one elbow propped on the gleaming countertop. Soft music flowed from the speakers, an Eric Clapton tune filling the room. Suddenly self-conscious in the wrinkled dress, Mimi yanked the bodice up a notch. Unfortunately the movement drew attention to the drooping neckline, instead of diverting it.

Seth sent the bartender a dark scowl. Mimi considered ordering a fancy drink, something sophisticated, but she refused to put on airs for Seth Broadhurst or any man. "Give me a light beer. Whatever you have on draft is fine."

The bartender's sideways grin irritated her while one of Seth's dark-blond eyebrows rose.

"And you, sir?"

Seth tapped his fingers on the counter. "Scotch on the rocks."

His gold-and-black-onyx ring flickered in the overhead light. A class ring from Harvard. "Figures."

"What?"

She hadn't realized she'd spoken out loud. "I said it figures you'd drink scotch. *Probably* the expensive stuff."

"There's nothing wrong with having class, Mimi."

Mimi indicated her beer. "Are you implying I don't?"

"No. Don't be so sensitive. You're analyzing everything I say, turning it into something it's not."

Regret pulled at Mimi. She was supposed to cheer him up. After all, he'd been nice to her the day Joey had been arrested. "I'm sorry, Seth. You deserve to drink whatever you want. I know it's been a bad day."

He seemed confused. "Why do you say that?"

"Well, er...watching Hannah marry someone else had to be hard."

The bartender handed him his drink, and he stared soulfully into the dark liquid, as if it held the answers to his problems. "I'm fine."

Mimi lifted her mug and took a small sip. "You don't have to pretend with me, Seth. I saw your face the day Hannah called off your wedding. And today..."

He met her gaze. "What about today?"

"Seeing Hannah marry someone else so soon after your breakup, well, you haven't had time to get over her. After all, you two dated a long time, and she's so great."

He nodded. "Yes, Hannah is a great lady. I want her to be happy, Mimi. I told her that."

"You deserve to be happy, too." Mimi patted his arm sympathetically. "Don't worry. You'll find someone else, Seth. Just don't let Hannah ruin you for another woman."

"Is that what you think?"

"I don't know. Hannah's a hard act to follow. I love her to death, but I've lived in her shadow all my life."

"Ahh."

"What does that mean?"

"Sibling rivalry."

"We're not rivals, so don't start that shrink stuff again. We're best friends."

Seth sipped his drink. "So you're not jealous of her?"

"Of course not. I'm proud of Hannah."

"Me, too. Hannah and I are friends." He sipped his drink. "You looked a little uncomfortable today, too, Mimi. Has Joey ruined *you* for another guy? Is that the reason you're against marriage?"

Mimi shrugged. "Like Grammy said, he was just a passing fancy."

Seth chuckled. "Easy come, easy go?"

"Something like that." Mimi traced a finger along the rim of her mug. "Although he did ask me to wait for him while he was in prison."

Seth's incredulous look made her laugh. "But you refused because you can't wait that long?"

"No, if I really loved someone, I could wait." She shuddered as Joey's arrest replayed in her mind. The humiliation. Her father's face on screen, the police, Joey holding Hannah at gunpoint. "He deceived me. My gosh, Seth, he cheated Dad and threatened Hannah. If anything had happened to them…"

"Your father and Hannah don't blame you." Seth covered her hand with his. His hand looked huge, but it felt warm, almost electric, sending strange sensations skittering up Mimi's spine. Feelings she didn't recognize.

"You do know that, don't you?" He tipped up her chin with his thumb.

"Yes, but I feel so stupid. I should have seen through Joey, done something to stop him—"

"Don't blame yourself, Mimi. Joey was a con artist. A pro. This wasn't the first time he'd deceived people."

"I still wish I'd caught on to his game."

"So what did you say when he asked you to wait for him?"

"To dream on."

Seth ran his knuckles over her cheek, his smile oddly tender. "Good for you. You can do better than him."

Mimi hesitated, studying him. "You really think so?"

Seth released her and turned his gaze back to his drink. Odd how cold she suddenly felt, as if losing that touch was important. Must be the chill from her damp dress.

"Sure," Seth said in a throaty voice. "He was a criminal. You're hardworking and honest and…"

"And what?"

"And beautiful."

Mimi almost choked on her drink. "You don't make that sound like a compliment."

"Beauty's great." Seth angled his head toward her. "As long as you have goals to go along with the looks."

"I have goals," Mimi said. "I told you I want to be an actress."

"Right."

Mimi's temper rose. "Okay, so I'm not a brain surgeon or a lawyer and I don't have a degree in anything, but I do have ambition. And I'm not settling for some two-bit loser like Joey again." Mimi glanced around the cozy bar. "I realize now that our relationship was just…physical."

A muscle ticked in Seth's jaw as if talking about physical intimacy made him uncomfortable. He obviously didn't specialize in sex therapy. "So, you know what you want in a guy next time?" he asked.

Mimi stewed over that question. "Maybe. Sort of."

"You don't sound sure."

"I'm sure of the qualities I *don't* want." Suddenly suspicious he might be using one of his psychiatrist tricks to lure her into spilling her secrets, she turned the tables on him. "What about you? What do you want in a relationship?"

"Someone to complement my lifestyle." His hand

tightened around his drink. Mimi watched his throat muscles work as he finished the drink, tension humming through the air. Boy, he had a nice neck, tanned and muscular.

She had to forget about his neck. "Let me guess. That would be someone steady, settled, a homemaker or another doctor, someone who'll fit into your routine?"

"You make me sound dull."

"I didn't mean it like that."

He narrowed his eyes.

"I meant you're dependable, steady, stable."

"You don't make those sound like compliments."

"No, they're great qualities. Just predictable."

He cleared his throat. "I'm not always predictable."

"Oh, yeah." Mimi let her gaze travel the length of him. "I bet you eat the same thing for breakfast every day. Get up at the exact same time every morning, even on weekends. Never go anywhere without your pocket calendar. Have sex once a week, Saturday night, 11:00 p.m., right after the news. You wear those old-fashioned white briefs, and you wouldn't be caught dead without an undershirt."

"Is that what Hannah told you?"

"Hannah never talked about your love life or underwear. She was always pretty private."

"Thank goodness for that."

"I'm right though, aren't I?"

"I refuse to talk about my love life with you." He squared his shoulders, his cheeks slightly red. "And as far as my underwear is concerned, you looked when that hope chest tore my pants.''

''I didn't have to look,'' Mimi said softly. She patted his arm, surprised at the rock-hard muscles bunching beneath his suit. ''It's all right to have a routine as long as you don't forget how to have fun, too.''

''And you're a connoisseur of a good time?''

Mimi shrugged. ''No date has ever accused me of being boring.''

''And there have been lots of dates, I suppose.''

''Enough.''

Seth ran his gaze over her. ''You're right, Mimi, I doubt you'd ever be accused of being boring.''

''What's that supposed to mean?''

''Just that you seem to enjoy stirring up things.''

Mimi bristled. ''Things?''

''Men.''

''Excuse me?''

''You know…'' He gestured at her hips. ''The way you walk.''

''What about the way I walk?''

''That little twitch thing you do with your hips. You kind of sway from side to side. And your legs…''

Mimi felt a smile coming on. The poor man was flustered. ''You don't like my legs, Seth?''

Seth chuckled sardonically. ''My God, your legs could be considered lethal weapons. Especially when you wear those miniskirts at the coffee shop.''

''So you've noticed my skirts?''

''It's hard not to. Every man in the place is staring

at you. Why do you think the café does such successful business?''

Mimi laughed mischievously. She should save Seth from himself, but she was having too much fun. ''I thought it was my 'hot brownie delight.''''

SETH UNDID the top button of his shirt. Hot brownie delight—jeez. It was her hot little body every man in the place wanted. Didn't she have any idea how appealing she was? He'd seen men order desserts just to finagle the chance to talk to her.

And how had their conversation turned to underwear and Mimi's dynamite legs?

He was supposed to be comforting her, not making a fool of himself by acting like the other lust-struck men in the place. And there were plenty.

Mimi was Hannah's little sister, and he felt compelled to protect her.

''Hey, Seth, they're playing a great dance number.''

Her green eyes sparkled in challenge, a snappy Ricky Martin tune drifting through the speakers. ''Wanna dance? No, let me guess, you don't.''

He didn't, but he'd be damned if he'd admit it. He reached for her hand and dragged her to the dance floor. ''I told you I'm not always predictable.''

Mimi's laughter was infectious and so were her moves. He tried to copy the sexy swaying of her hips and body, and found himself transfixed by the heat in her eyes. One button, then two, came undone on his jacket as he strove for air on the crowded dance floor. When the fast song ended, Faith Hill's sexy voice purred out the slow tune "Breathe." He took Mimi in his arms and they swayed together, her body pressed intimately into the hard planes of his, her breath whispering against his neck. His heart pounded as her breasts pressed against him.

Seth tried to stifle his body's reaction, but that damned perfume of hers invaded his senses, turning his brain into a fuzzy mess, his body into a hard, aching ball of need.

They danced until the lights dimmed, until the music stopped, as if both of them were prolonging the evening, avoiding going to the room.

"I'm hungry," Mimi said, her slender hand curled on his chest. "Let's take some dessert and coffee to the room."

He cupped the back of her neck with his hand, gently massaging the area. "Sounds good to me."

She ordered a hot fudge sundae, along with strawberries and whipped cream, and he led her toward the elevator, the sounds of the staff's voices echoing from the deserted bar behind them. Tension hummed through the dark hotel room as they entered. Rich oak furniture filled the space, plush carpeting blanketed the floors, a Jacuzzi in the corner drew his eye, and a single king-size bed draped in gold velvet loomed in the middle.

It would be a mistake to share that bed. Sleeping with Mimi was never in the plans. Not an option.

So why did he suddenly feel obsessed with the idea?

He drank his coffee, instead. He'd never thought eating especially sexual, just a routine necessary for life functions—until he watched Mimi devour the hot fudge sundae, licking the sauce from her luscious lips, making him itch to lick her mouth, too. Mimi's eyes darkened with a raw hunger, the sort he'd never seen in Hannah's eyes. Or in any woman's eyes—not when they were looking at him.

"You don't want your strawberries?" Mimi asked with a teasing smile.

He shrugged, the urge to tease her overriding his common sense. He didn't want to be dull, predictable Seth anymore. "I want the whipped cream."

She laughed, dipped her finger into the dessert and held it up. He saw the challenge in her eyes again. And something else.

Passion.

The excitement of a woman wanting a man. The realization they were stranded together in a romantic hotel in a blizzard, alone for the very first time. A man and woman who had just felt the contours of each other's bodies, who had just shared a few comforting moments and a dance that had stirred wicked fantasies, who had an unexpected heat simmering between them.

Mimi was right—he was boring. Dull. Predictable.

He had never done anything impetuous. Or exciting.

But he wanted to now.

He wanted to do something wicked, naughty. Maybe shocking.

He flicked out his tongue, licked the whipped cream from her finger and saw her dress stretch taut across her breasts. The touch of her finger on his mouth taunted him, made him realize he wanted Mimi, wanted her so badly he could barely breathe. Wanted just once to taste her passion, to know what it felt like to delve into that sweet, tantalizing body and hold her through the night, to feel alive.

Disgusted with his white underwear and his pocket calendar and undershirts, he reached out and, for the first time in his life, took something off-limits, something for himself, something only for the moment.

He drew Mimi into his arms and kissed her.

Chapter Four

Mimi closed her eyes and threw caution to the wind as she sank into Seth's strong arms. The taste of whipped cream, scotch and coffee mingled with the heady scent of passion, driving her into sweet oblivion. Why had she ever thought this man dull? Or predictable?

She'd certainly never imagined Seth would seduce her, especially with such hunger. He had a great ear for listening and it was even better for kissing, she thought, nibbling at his earlobe. And his hands... They found all the secret erogenous areas of her body—her neck, the sensitive spot behind her ear, the curve of her shoulder blade, the tips of her breasts—and he tormented her with gentle strokes that were so sensual she found herself groping for the buttons on his shirt. A small smattering of dark blond hair peeked from the opening, and his muscular arms enveloped her as he backed her toward the bed.

Seth was smart and handsome, a man to be admired, and he wanted *her*—Mimi Hartwell, the misfit kid who always seemed to screw up things, the girl without a degree or a fancy job title. Delicious sensations skated through her as she remembered his hard body swaying against hers when they'd danced. He'd held her as if she were a piece of fine china that might break, something to treasure and care for. So unlike the way Joey had held her or the way any other man had ever treated her.

With a groan that sent a shiver up her spine, he threaded his hand through her hair, drawing her closer so she could feel his arousal, so she could hear his harsh breathing, so she could sense the loneliness in his soul. She met his hunger with her tongue and her heart, determined to erase any sadness lingering from the past.

There was some reason she shouldn't be doing this, she thought vaguely, hesitating for a second as he deepened the kiss. It was something to do with Hannah… No, Hannah was married now, on her honeymoon. She was here in this dimly lit romantic haven, snow falling outside, the whisper of winter swirling around them, and Seth was hot…so hot. And so tender.

They fell to the bed in a tangle of arms and legs and heated moans. Mimi had never felt such a pull to be close to someone. Seth cupped her face and gazed into her eyes. "We shouldn't do this."

"I know."

His hands pulled her closer, stroked her inner thigh. "It's probably not a good idea."

"But it feels so good, Seth, so right." She traced a finger along his jaw, mesmerized by the moonlight spilling onto his face, shading his broad jaw with sharp angles and planes, darkening his eyes to black.

Eyes that whispered their yearning in the quiet of the night. She slid the gown down and dropped it to the floor. A smile curved her mouth when she saw the appreciation in his gaze. His skin, translucent and glowing with the faint hint of excitement, felt warm to her fingertips as he stripped his shirt off.

He held her face between his hands. "You are beautiful, Mimi. God, I can't believe I'm here like this with you."

"And I take back what I said. You're not dull at all." She lifted her hand and swept it through his hair, her heart pounding as he lowered his head and dropped kisses along her neck, then lower. His breath bathed her body, his whispered words of desire stoked the fire between them, and his hands drove her over the edge. The flames sizzled, chasing away the earlier chill from the snowstorm, the lingering embers of hesitation dying with each breath and kiss. And when he joined his body with hers, they rode the crest of the wave together and found ecstasy in each other's arms.

SOMETIME AFTER his internal clock would have woken him in the morning, Seth awoke from the most satisfying dream he'd ever had to find a delicious, tantalizing body draped across him. Long, wild, curly auburn hair lay across his chest, and a pair of long, sexy legs were wedged between his own. Although his muscles were sore from his fall, his body stirred to life again and he sighed with bliss, unable to believe he still had the energy to want this woman. After all, they'd already made love countless times.

Countless?

He mentally ticked off the different places they'd found pleasure—the bed, the shower, the bed, the Jacuzzi, the bed again.

His heart thundered in his chest as he took another mental count of the number of condoms he'd had in his wallet—the ones he'd carried for two years just to be prepared in case he and Hannah ever...

No, he couldn't think about Hannah while lying in bed with her sister.

Dear God. The math didn't add up. He'd had four condoms. They'd made love five times. And sometime during the night, he remembered Mimi saying she wasn't on the pill.

He slapped his forehead, pride for his male prowess and foreboding for the possible consequences warring within his chest. One eye darted toward the vixen who'd stirred his blood and passion to life. Her long eyelashes fluttered, and a sweet little smile curved her lips. Beautiful was too blasé a word for Mimi.

Other words came to mind—ravenous, sensational, creative, exciting, impulsive...off-limits.

He groaned and tried to lift her from his body, gritting his teeth when his body swelled, aching for her again. Ethics, common sense and his friendship with Hannah aside, it had been a cataclysmic night. But a huge mistake.

Sure, they'd had great sex, but that could have been the liquor talking. Except he'd only had one drink. And if he remembered correctly, so had Mimi.

What had possessed them? The wedding, getting stranded, the heat in the car, all that damn dancing?

He'd never go dancing again.

How would he face Hannah at the hospital? Worse, what would Mimi expect now? One night with her was great, but a relationship... No, they were too different.

Their career paths were on very different courses. They didn't associate with the same type of people. He was practical, conservative; she was impractical, showy. He owned a traditional home, worked with scholarly types, had to live up to his family's expectations and their place in society. Mimi was anything but traditional, cavorted with a wild crowd, often appeared on her father's wacky commercials. Good God, they'd only wound up together because of Hannah. And if Hannah found out he'd slept with her sister, she might think he'd used Mimi to get over her.

No, he and Mimi were disastrous together. Their earlier conversation rose to haunt him. The only thing they had in common was that neither wanted marriage or kids. At least not now.

But what if she was pregnant?

MIMI SQUEEZED her eyes shut, pretending sleep as she wrestled with the awkward morning after. She knew Seth was awake, had felt his heart start pounding double time and his muscles tense, as if he, too, didn't know quite how to handle things. His lower body didn't seem to be listening to his brain, though. If she moved an inch to either side, they would have a repeat of the night before—only now, in the light of day, it didn't seem like such a great idea.

When would she learn not to be so impetuous?

Seth gently pulled her arms from around his neck, and she allowed him to roll her to the side. She emitted a little moan as if she might be stirring from slumber to make the act seem more real—after all, she was an actress. She could pretend nothing had happened and blow the whole night off with a shrug if he really weirded out on her.

She curled on her side, dragging the satin sheets over her as he padded barefoot to the bathroom. But she couldn't resist peeking through a slitted eye to admire his firm, muscular backside. Good grief, the man had great buns and a broad back, and corded muscles she hadn't expected. Why did he hide them under those boring gray suits?

Because he was a psychiatrist, she reminded herself, crashing back to reality. The very reason the two of them did not belong together. She was the impulsive, middle-class, college-dropout child of wacky Wiley Hartwell; he was the genius-doctor son of the upper-class Broadhursts.

She heard the shower kick on, remembered the two of them and all the naughty things they'd done beneath the water, the look on Seth's face when she'd gotten inventive with strawberries—they'd tasted sinful wedged in his navel with a dash of lime juice—and felt an odd kind of loneliness. The night had been spectacular. He had held her and loved her more tenderly than any man ever had. Did it really have to end? Maybe she'd shortchanged herself into thinking she didn't deserve someone as sophisticated as Seth.

Then she noticed the rumpled bridesmaid dress, and desire drained from her faster than dishwater drained from a sink. She'd stooped lower than ever—she had broken the unspoken rule about not dating a sister's former boyfriend. Disgust filled her. She'd always walked in Hannah's shadow, and she'd never really minded. Hadn't minded wearing her hand-me-down clothes or shoes or even sharing a room with her when she was growing up.

But she absolutely drew the line at taking her leftover men.

SETH EMERGED from the steamy bathroom and hissed in frustration at his torn pants. Then he saw Mimi.

Gut-wrenchingly beautiful, Mimi jumped from the bed, twisting the sheet around her naked body. The satin fabric molded to every curve and peak, accentuating her lush figure so he could almost see her skin through the thin layer of cloth. Her wild hair spiraled around her bare shoulders in a tangle, her cheeks were flushed, her eyes heavy-lidded with sleep, her makeup faded. But tousled and freshly loved, she looked more appealing than ever.

Only, where passion and ecstasy had glistened in her eyes last night, turmoil now stretched across her features. She looked miserable, which made him feel even more miserable. Hadn't she enjoyed their night together? He'd certainly thought so.

"This was a mistake," they said in unison.

"We shouldn't have, you know," Mimi said in a wobbly voice.

"It was my fault. I...I was only trying to comfort you about Joey—"

"*You* were trying to comfort *me?*"

He tried to think of a better way to phrase his concerns.

Then she threw him for a loop. "I was trying to comfort you over Hannah."

His mouth tightened. Had she made love to him out of some misguided pity? "I don't need your help getting over Hannah."

"And I don't need you giving me therapy over Joey."

"Fine, this…us…it won't happen again."

"Absolutely not."

"We'll act like it *never* happened."

"Right. And we won't tell anyone."

His temper flared. She'd never seemed secretive about that hood DeLito. Their public displays of affection had been almost embarrassing. "I'm certainly not going to advertise it."

She nodded. "You won't tell Hannah?" Genuine horror rang in her voice.

"Of course I won't tell Hannah. After all, I still have to work with her."

"And she's *my* sister."

Her chin wobbled as if she was on the verge of tears, and his gut clenched. He reached for her, the regret in his heart almost as dark as the look she gave him. "I'll check the weather conditions if you want to shower."

"Fine. Oh, and you might want to put some powder on that eye. It's a little blue." Mimi swept the wrinkled bridesmaid dress from the floor and stumbled toward the bathroom. Seth's stomach knotted as his body reacted, itching to go with her.

Of course he didn't move. He kept his feet glued to the floor. In fact, his fingers tightened around the empty condom packet. He'd been on the verge of discussing their possible problem when he'd seen her chin wobble. Maybe he'd save that conversation for the car. Once they were driving, she couldn't just run away.

MIMI PRAYED the soap and water and steam would clear her head and bring her back to her senses. As much as she didn't want to *want* Seth again, when she'd seen him standing there, all shirtless and long brawny limbs, tight-lipped and sad eyed, she'd wanted to wipe that tightness off his face and that sadness out of his eyes and make him remember how great the night had been. She wanted to make him laugh and purr her name in that husky voice he'd used in the wee hours of the morning.

But he thought their lovemaking was a mistake and so did she, and then there was Hannah, and oh, God...

Tears leaked from her eyes and she let them fall onto the shower floor, unable to stop the flood. She always seemed to be creating messes.

First, when she was little, she'd been so klutzy and messy she'd driven her own mother away. Grammy had said she was creative, and her father had laughed and bragged about her projects, but her mother had hated all the glue, glitter, paints, costumes and cooking disasters. She'd constantly complained, but Mimi had argued that her dad loved her impromptu shows, that he always ate her concoctions, no matter how bizarre they sounded. As a teenager, she'd brought home stray animals, and once she'd saved a turtle, but it smelled so badly her mother had gotten ill. Then her mother had walked out. And it was all her fault.

Her teenage years had been rocky, too—she'd bounced from one loser boyfriend to another. Then she'd dropped out of college to pursue an acting career. And this past year she'd hooked up with Joey. He'd seemed like a loner when he'd first come to Sugar Hill, and she'd fallen for his candy-coated compliments. She'd been so naive she hadn't known he was dating her to steal from her father. She'd put her father, his business and Hannah in danger because she'd been too impulsive and trusting.

And now she'd really lost her mind. She'd taken Hannah's ex-boyfriend to bed and actually imagined… No, she was not going to even entertain the possibility they might have a relationship. He had to get back to his analyzing and his stuffy family, and she had to return to her job as a manager of the café and practice for the audition.

Finally her tears subsided. She toweled off and yanked on the bridesmaid dress, feeling like a fool wearing a rumpled evening outfit at seven in the morning. Her only comfort was that no one would ever know she and Seth had been together.

Minutes later she patted her cheeks to put some color into them, and hoped Seth didn't notice her red, puffy eyes. He was completely dressed, his jacket buttoned to hide the tear in his slacks, his body as stiff as a marble wall as he stood by the door. He watched her steadily, his expression closed.

She lifted her chin and asked, "Ready?"

He nodded. "Mimi—"

"No, don't." She held up a warning hand. "Nothing happened. And no one will ever know. Agreed?"

He hesitated and her heart did a strange pitter-patter. Finally he said in a low voice, "Agreed."

She nodded, wondering if the roads were clear enough to drive, but decided not to ask. They couldn't possibly stay in the hotel a moment longer. Determined not to become emotional, she opened the door, only to see a couple who looked exactly like Hannah and Jake walking down the hallway of the hotel. Their hushed voices drifted toward her from the elevator, and her stomach churned.

The couple *was* Hannah and Jake.

Chapter Five

Seth started to go into the hall, but Mimi yanked him back inside the room and slammed the door. Did she want to talk? Do something else? Had she changed her mind about not repeating their—

"Hannah and Jake are in the hall!"

"They're *here?*"

Mimi nodded, looking horrified. "I had no idea."

"Me, neither."

They leaned against the door as if to bar it in case Hannah had seen them and might come blasting through. Tension thrummed between them.

"I suppose they couldn't get to the airport because of the bad weather," Seth said, trying to think logically.

"The flights were probably canceled."

"And the roads going to the interstate were closed."

"And this was the only hotel with a vacancy."

Their gazes caught, and he noticed Mimi's puffy and swollen eyes. "Good Lord, you've been crying. What's wrong?" He was so shocked his knees wobbled. Hannah hadn't been the emotional type, and neither was his mother. Of course when some of his patients got hysterical, he prescribed sedatives for them. But he couldn't offer Mimi sedatives, not with the possibility of a pregnancy.

She quickly averted her gaze. "I just felt sappy with Hannah getting married and Mom coming back, and I'm having PMS and...sex relieves tension."

He couldn't help but smile at her blunt honesty. Tenderness for her filled him. Hannah had been only nine when her mother deserted them, so Mimi would have been seven. It must have been a traumatic time for all of them. "How do you feel about your mother's return?"

"Stop with the shrink stuff, already." With a stubborn glare, she grabbed the doorknob. "I wonder if they've gone."

The scent of her perfume clung to her dress, tormenting him with reminders of their evening together, but her perfect pink mouth was pressed into a tight line, and her posture clearly indicated she wanted distance between them. She obviously was even more concerned about Hannah knowing they'd slept together than he was. He felt stung. "You want us to leave separately and meet at the car?"

"That's probably a good idea."

He nodded tightly. "All right. You go ahead. I'll meet you in about five minutes."

Her dress swished noisily as she pulled open the door and peered out. When the coast was clear, she darted into the hallway, dangling her pink heels in one hand, yanking at the drooping bodice of the dress with the other, then bypassed the elevator and hurried into the stairwell. He glanced out the window and finally saw her emerge from the hotel a few minutes later. She stopped, leaned against a post and stuffed her feet into her shoes. Wobbling on her heels, she wove through the trees bordering the hotel like a thief in the night and headed toward his Lexus at a dead run.

MIMI LEANED against the car to catch her breath while she glanced around the crowded lot, grateful for the trees bordering the property. She didn't think anyone had seen her, although she'd noticed a couple of reporters in the lobby, obviously interviewing stranded motorists for a story on the blizzard. Thank heavens they hadn't spotted her.

Seconds later Seth walked down the snow-dusted drive, his hands in his pockets, his face stoic as he gazed around at the ice-heavy branches of the trees. He looked handsome and calm and totally in control. Unaffected by their night together. The complete opposite of her.

Damn him.

He hit the release on his key and opened the door for her—a real gentlemen—and she scooted under his arm and practically dived into the car. He climbed in, switched on the ignition and turned to look at her. "I don't think anyone saw us together."

She breathed a sigh of relief. "Thank God."

He turned on the radio, then pulled down the drive. "I stopped at the desk to ask about the roads. Apparently the plows were out early, so I think we can get through."

''We have to,'' Mimi said, her skirt crinkling noisily as she twisted the material in her lap.

Several minutes passed, tension building as they slowly wound down the mountain road. A few icy patches looked hazardous, and Mimi held her breath as Seth expertly steered the car around them. When they finally turned onto the interstate, he cleared his throat.

''We have to talk,'' he said in a dark voice.

''I think we already said everything we need to say.''

''I don't think so.'' He reached into his pocket and lay an empty foil packet in the middle of the console, the shiny paper glowing like a red neon sign.

Mimi instantly reached out her hand to cover it as if the few people daring enough to brave the roads this morning could see into the car and would know exactly what had transpired between them. ''What are you doing?''

''I'm trying to tell you something.''

''I know what they are,'' Mimi said through gritted teeth.

''Did you take a count of how many we used?''

''What? You mean did I count the number of times we... Well, no. But it was a lot.'' She was sore in spots where she had never been sore before.

He clenched his hands around the steering wheel. ''Well, I did. And I came up short.''

Of course he would count. He was practical, logical, rational Seth Broadhurst. Mimi felt a sinking sensation in her stomach as she realized the direction of his conversation—the topic was much more frightening than the icy roads. "You mean we…forgot one time?"

"I believe it was in the Jacuzzi."

"All those bubbles…" Mimi said, distracted by the memory. "We were so carried away…"

"I've *never* gotten carried away and forgotten before." He rubbed a hand along his neck, sounding disgusted. She wasn't sure if it was because he'd gotten carried away or because they'd forgotten or because of the possible consequences. His hand snaked over hers. "You will let me know if anything happens, won't you, Mimi?"

"I…it'll be fine. I'm…I'm sure."

He shot her an uncertain look.

"Well, almost sure. I told you I was PMSing."

His eyes darkened. "I will take full responsibility if…you know, if something happens."

Of course he would take responsibility, whether he liked it or not. Noble, nice, responsible Seth, exactly as Hannah had always described, except for the sex part. Hannah—dear God, what would she tell her sister if she wound up pregnant with Seth's baby? "Nothing is going to happen."

He arched a brow at her clipped tone. "Just promise me you'll tell me."

Mimi dropped her head into her hands, a headache pinching at her temples. "But you don't want kids."

"Neither do you."

"I won't get pregnant."

He said nothing, simply stared at her. "Promise me you'll tell me, anyway."

Mimi sighed. "Okay. But it's not going to happen.'' The memory of her hope chest floated through her mind—the baby blanket and rattle.

She clutched her stomach, feeling nauseous. No, the items in her hope chest had been placed there by mistake, just like the incredible night with Seth had been a mistake. Neither one meant anything. They weren't an omen of the future as Hannah's hope chest had been. Her future involved acting and TV and…other men.

As soon as she returned to Sugar Hill, to her own apartment with her dog and cat, everything would return to normal. She'd simply hit the fast erase button in her mind. And nobody would ever have to know she and Seth had spent the night together.

"IS THIS WHAT I think it is?

Mimi stared in horror at the newspaper Alison held in her hands. A color photo showed her and Seth, looking dreamy-eyed and glued together as they headed toward their hotel room. At least the story wasn't on the front page. And she and Seth weren't really the focus of the picture; they were actually in the background. Obviously the reporter had been interviewing a couple from New Jersey stranded on their way to the beach, and he'd caught them in the photo.

So much for nobody finding out she and Seth had been together.

"Mimi, is it?"

"Er…no, not exactly."

Alison plopped onto Mimi's bright yellow U-shaped sofa with a paper bag, then pulled out bagels and coffee. "What does that mean?"

Mimi scratched her dog's ears while she scanned the article. Some stranded guests had spent the night in a local school cafeteria, others at churches, when they couldn't find hotels. The reporter listed the couples' names. At least he hadn't identified her or Seth.

"Come on, you might as well tell me," Alison said matter-of-factly. "Maybe I can help cushion things for Dad."

"He's going to freak and think I'm totally irresponsible, especially after I was so stupid with Joey."

"Are you going to tell Hannah?" Alison sighed and stirred sugar into her coffee. Mimi left hers unsweetened and tore off a tiny piece of bagel for Wrangler, her pug, and another piece for Esmereldo, the stray cat she'd taken in the week before. "No, I don't want Hannah to find out. Since she's out of town, maybe she won't see it."

Alison studied her and Mimi squirmed. "Oh, my gosh. You actually slept with him, didn't you?"

Mimi nodded miserably, the horror of what she'd done escalating. "It…it just happened. One minute I was comforting him over losing Hannah and he was talking to me about Joey, then he started looking at me funny, all hot and sexy and *different*, and I challenged him to dance because I didn't think he would, and he did. And it was dark and he's actually quite muscular under those suits, and the music was so romantic and he was so tender, exciting kind of tender, not like Joey, and he isn't boring like I thought he'd be."

Alison blew into her coffee. "Good Lord, Mimi."

"I know." Mimi moaned and folded her legs Indian-style on the couch. "It was because we were stranded, sharing those close quarters. We tried to get two rooms, honest."

"I thought you didn't even like Seth. Remember the things you said to Hannah when she was engaged to him? That she might be dreaming about sleeping with another man because Seth wasn't the kind of man to elicit fantasies."

"I know." Mimi dropped her head forward into her hand. "But he was different last night. *Way* different."

They sat silently, sipping their coffee. Alison tore a bagel in half and offered part of it to Mimi, but Mimi declined, her throat too full of disgust to swallow food.

"So are you two an item now?"

Mimi nearly spilled her coffee on Esmereldo. "No. We agreed it was a mistake. It won't happen again." She shuddered. "But it gets worse, Ali. Jake and Hannah were at the hotel."

"Did they see you?"

"No, I ducked out a side door and Seth followed later."

Alison sighed. "Good. Not that I don't want you to be happy if you want Seth, sis, but it is kind of awkward since he and Hannah were almost married."

"Don't you think I know that? I still can't believe I actually did the wild thing with him."

Alison arched a brow, her mouth quirked sideways. "So it was wild, huh?"

Mimi grinned in spite of herself. "Wilder than I'd ever imagined."

"Hmm. Then maybe you should go out with him and see where this thing goes. Maybe—"

"No, we've never dated each other's boyfriends before."

"Seth is an ex-boyfriend."

"Ex or not, we've never done that and I don't intend to start." Mimi gestured toward the photograph. "Do you think anyone will recognize us? I mean, I do have my back to the camera, and you can't really see Seth's face that clearly."

"You're right. I recognized you because of the dress."

Mimi felt glum again. "Yeah, that bridesmaid dress is pretty obvious."

"But look on the bright side. Hannah's out of town on her honeymoon and won't be back until next week, so she won't see the paper. By then, the news will be old."

Mimi nodded. "Maybe Dad won't read the paper, either."

"Dad always reads the paper. He's compulsive about checking his new ad for the week."

"Great. He'll probably knock on the door any minute."

"Maybe he'll be so busy at work he won't have time. And I think he was meeting Mom for lunch."

"What's that all about?"

Alison shrugged. "I don't know. I still can't believe she came to the wedding."

"I'm glad for Hannah's sake, but it was a shock," Mimi said, shifting restlessly. "Did you talk to her?"

"No." Alison picked at a chipped fingernail, looking troubled. "At least, I tried not to. But she made it a point to catch me in the corner."

"She tried to do the same to me, but I cracked a joke and escaped. What did she want?"

"You won't believe it."

"What?"

"She's setting up a law practice here in Sugar Hill."

Mimi's heart raced. "She's moving here permanently?"

Alison nodded and placed her empty coffee cup on the table. "Right down the street from your coffee shop."

"I can't believe it. Does she know you're looking at renting the space adjoining mine?"

"Apparently so. She asked the real-estate agent about it, but Verna told her I'd already put it on hold. Then she looked at the space on the other side of you, but it was too big."

"Thank heavens."

Alison pulled at a loose string on her sweater. "You want to know the real clincher?"

"What?"

"She offered to lend me money to start my business."

"Unbelievable."

Alison began to pace. "I know. It's not fair. She disappears from our lives for years, then suddenly waltzes home and wants to jump right back in as if nothing happened.''

The coffee curdled in Mimi's stomach. Her mother had married their father because she'd been pregnant with Hannah, but their marriage had ended in disaster. What if... No, she wouldn't think about the possibility. At least she had a few good memories of their mom, though. Alison had hardly any. ''What did you tell her when she offered you the loan?''

''I told her she'd never been in my life before, and I didn't need her now.''

Mimi rose from the sofa, gently put the cat on the floor and hugged Alison. ''My sentiments exactly. We've got each other and Hannah and Dad and Grammy Rose. That's all the family we need.'' Her gaze fell to the newspaper and she sighed. She'd do anything for her family, anything to keep them from being hurt.

Even if that meant keeping her secret about Seth from Hannah and never seeing him again.

Chapter Six

Seth had a bad feeling the entire way home. The feeling grew worse when he discovered his parents' black Cadillac parked at the curb by his house. His anxiety magnified a hundredfold when his father climbed from the car, waving a newspaper with a color photo of him and Mimi entering an elevator in Magnolia Manor. A potted plant shielded most of his face, but his Harvard ring gleamed in the background. Mimi, with her wild auburn hair and that killer body, would have been recognizable anywhere. Especially wearing that hot-pink bridesmaid dress.

"What do you mean by this?" his father asked.

His mother gasped. "And what happened to your face? You look like you've been in a brawl."

Seth rubbed a hand over the bruise around his eye, remembering the tumble with Mimi. He grinned in spite of himself. "I had a little fall. No big deal."

"Please tell me you haven't hooked up with that heathen Hartwell girl." Mrs. Broadhurst fluttered a hand in front of her forehead as if she might faint at the appalling idea.

Seth's temper flared. "She is not a heathen, Mother. Don't be so dramatic."

"My God, you have hooked up with her," his father said in an accusing tone.

"Dating the other one was tolerable—at least she was a doctor," his mother continued, "but after humiliating you in front of the whole town, how can you even consider seeing her sister? Why, the gossip has barely died down from the first debacle. Now you want to start another?"

"Thanks, Mom. I hope you're not on the sunshine committee for the hospital. You really know how to make a person feel better."

His father slapped the paper against his hand. "Have you considered what publicity like this might do to your reputation at the hospital?"

Seth gritted his teeth and pushed past his parents to open his front door. "I'm not worried about my reputation. And who I see is none of your concern. I'm an adult."

"You certainly aren't acting like one," his mother said. "Not if you're cavorting with women like *her*."

"What's that supposed to mean?" Seth asked, irritated when his parents followed him inside.

"So you *are* seeing her?"

"No. I..." Seth bit back the words, refusing to give them an explanation. "You don't have to insult Mimi."

"Why not? She's always in the paper with her dad. That man's the biggest spectacle in Sugar Hill," his mother said.

"And she was dating that hoodlum from her father's dealership. They might all be crooks."

"Mimi was cleared," Seth said. "She had no idea DeLito was a thief. She feels terrible about the whole episode."

His mother waved her hand again. "I can't believe you're actually defending her."

"I'm telling you the truth." Seth folded his arms and faced them, his pulse hammering. "If Mimi is guilty of anything, it's of being too trusting."

His mother leaned against the sofa table, sending the crystal vase into a wobble. "She's a hussy."

"She is not."

"Need I remind you she's a waitress in a coffee shop," Mr. Broadhurst said. "She's simply not on your level."

He and Mimi had certainly been on the same level the night before in bed, but he refused to be goaded. "Mimi's not just a waitress, she manages the place," Seth said. "And you two are snobs."

His mother's heels clicked as she stomped toward the door, her nose in the air, her head thrust back like an angry ostrich. "I don't know what she did to you—probably put you under some kind of spell," Mrs. Broadhurst said. "But one evening with her, and you're not the same man. You've lost all respect for your family."

She was right—he was a different man. A sexually sated, happy man who'd been in total ecstasy only hours after his former fiancée had married another man. All thanks to Mimi.

"Look, son," Mr. Broadhurst said, "I know a man

has needs. If you want...you know, sex, for God's sake, at least find a woman who doesn't flaunt her picture in the paper all the time like these Hartwells.''

Seth fisted his hands. "Mimi didn't know about the picture," he snapped. "She's a nice girl."

His father ignored Seth's comment as he slammed the door behind him. Seth collapsed onto his gray leather sofa and glanced around his living room, irritation and worry burning through his veins. Mimi didn't want anyone to know they'd been together.

He wondered if she'd seen the newspaper.

THE SUGAR HILL CAFÉ was fairly quiet, Mimi thought, save for her own occasional self-chatter. "Why did you sleep with Seth Broadhurst? You're a fool, Mimi Hartwell. What if you do wind up...?"

She dumped a cup of cocoa into the rich batter and stirred vigorously. She'd already tried three different variations, but each had failed, and now she was obsessing about whether to add more peanut-butter chips or butterscotch.

Anything to help her forget that revealing newspaper photo. Better to obsess about a recipe than whether or not Hannah might have found out about her and Seth. Or whether she might turn up pregnant. Or whether Seth had seen the newspaper. Or whether Seth was comparing their lovemaking to the times he'd been with Hannah. Not that Hannah had mentioned their sex life.

The last thought had bulldozed into her mind and sent her to work an hour ago to keep busy. Even though she'd told herself it didn't matter—she wasn't competing with Hannah, and surely Seth was too much of a gentlemen to compare the sisters—she still couldn't let the matter go. Besides, Hannah was happily married, and Mimi didn't intend to sleep with Seth again or be with him in any way, shape or form. She wasn't going to obsess about Hannah or Seth or their nonrelationship anymore. She would not even give the man a thought.

Except the rich chocolate did remind her of the dessert they'd shared in the hotel. The way he'd tasted all warm and sexy. She licked the spoon, savoring the sensation of chocolate batter on her tongue and remembering the hot way Seth had looked at her when he'd licked the whipped cream off her finger.

Furious with herself, Mimi emptied the batter into the baking pan, popped it into the oven and peeked from the kitchen. Except for Penny and Chris, the two teenagers who helped out on Saturdays, the coffee shop was empty. The young couple stood hunched together, laughing as they sipped café mochas, obviously in love. Simple for them. Not for her and Seth.

The bell chimed above the doorway, and her father walked in, carrying the Saturday paper under his arm. Mimi sighed and braced herself for his questions.

NORMALLY SETH DIDN'T schedule appointments on Saturday, but one of the single parents from his divorce group had called, sounding troubled, so he'd told her to meet him at one o'clock. Anything to keep his mind off Mimi and the night before. And the way they'd parted.

He had a feeling Mimi wouldn't call him if she

discovered she was pregnant. She'd certainly acted as if it would be the last time she'd ever see him.

His methodical mind kicked in. On one level, the thought of not seeing Mimi again, or any of the Hartwells, seemed like a good idea. He needed to move on with his life. He had to live up to his position at the hospital, the expectations of his parents. He tapped his pen on the desk, thinking of the numerous lectures his father had given him. His father's father had wiled away all the family money, so Seth's dad had grown up near poverty. Intelligence, hard work and determination had been the key to his dad's escape from a destitute life. Not wanting his son to suffer the same fate, he'd given Seth the finest education money could buy. Seth understood it was his duty not to let down his family. His intelligence had been a gift. And he wanted to use it to help others.

Mimi's face flashed into his mind. He'd started out wanting to help her. But then things had gotten out of hand.

He knew they were wrong for each other. But would he ever again experience the mind-numbing feelings he'd had when he'd held Mimi in his arms, when they'd made love? He and Hannah had never had that wild physical spark between them, the very reason they'd never really moved past the platonic stage, despite their engagement. Not so with Mimi. The chemistry was there, but they had nothing else in common.

A knock on the door jerked him from his thoughts, and he invited Delores Flat to come in and sit down. She got straight to the problem. ''Georgie's asking about his father again. He wants to know why he didn't show up to take him to the ball game like he promised.'' She ran a hand over her necklace, the pearls clicking as she stroked them. ''It was easy to pacify Georgie when he was little. But now that he's getting older, he doesn't buy the excuses I make up.''

''Have you tried telling him the truth?''

''What? That his father doesn't care about him? That he never wanted to be a part of his life?''

Seth swallowed. If Mimi was pregnant and decided not to include him in her life, what would she tell their child? Although taking responsibility for a baby of his own scared him, he would never let her bring up the child alone. He'd seen enough kids suffer because of broken families.

''Dr. Broadhurst, what should I do?''

Seth shook himself. ''That's not what I meant. Perhaps your husband does care, but he doesn't realize how much he's hurting your son.''

''I've sure as hell tried to tell him.''

Seth frowned. ''Let me talk to Ralph.''

Mrs. Flat's fingers jerked on the necklace. ''What should I do in the meantime? Ralph says he'll pick up Georgie, but sometimes he doesn't show up at all.''

Seth steepled his fingers together. ''Focus on the fact that his dad is busy and that he does love him, but he isn't always dependable. Explain that adults have flaws, too. We don't want Georgie to think his father's absence is his fault.''

''No, no, I don't want that.'' Tears seeped from her eyes. ''It's just that I feel so alone. No one understands how hard it is to be both mother and father to little Georgie.''

Although every situation varied, Seth had heard the same comment from other single parents. "Look, Mrs. Flat, I'm forming a support group for single parents, and I'd like you to come. It'll be a chance to meet other men and women facing similar problems.''

Seth glanced at his calendar. "I'll let you know when the first meeting will be. Maybe you can get Ralph to come, too.'' He scribbled a reminder to phone her husband and urge him to attend.

The woman finally dropped her hand from her pearls and stood. "All right, Dr. Broadhurst. Let me know the time and place and I'll be there.''

Seth watched her leave, his mind sorting through the details. He'd need a relaxed place for the meeting, maybe one of the rooms in the community center neighboring the hospital, a few chairs, some food. A plan formed in his head. Mimi's café was near the hospital. She catered most of the hospital functions. Maybe he'd hire her to cater the informal gathering. After all, it would be the perfect excuse to keep an eye on her—and any other developments that might pop up from their night together.

MIMI SETTLED into a corner booth with her father, two pieces of chocolate cheesecake between them, well aware her father had that worried look on his face. But she was an actress, so she plastered on a cheery smile.

"Are you all right, honey?''

Mimi sipped her cappuccino. "Yep. I'm working

on a new recipe. Something even better than that mudslinger pie.''

Wiley's eyes lit up. ''That's my favorite. My gosh, you can cook, honey.''

''It was all those easy-bake ovens you got me when I was little.'' She patted her dad's hand. ''Thanks for being so tolerant, Dad. You were great to put up with my messes.''

''Honey, you've always been so much fun. I enjoyed watching you be creative.'' Wiley cut into his cheesecake, his gaze darting to the newspaper on the table.

Mimi's stomach did a flip-flop. ''You obviously saw the picture.''

He chewed thoughtfully. ''You know, I never put the two of you together, but I can see it now. Seth's a fine man.''

''What?''

''Sure.'' His dark eyes rested on her. ''Seth's a fine man. I always liked him when he was dating Hannah.''

Mimi winced.

''Sorry. I didn't mean to bring that up, but I wondered if you'd had a thing for him while they were dating.''

Mimi's cup clattered on the saucer. ''Of course not.''

Wiley shrugged. ''Doesn't matter now, sweetheart. Hannah's happily married. And I wanted you to know I approve.''

''You approve?''

''Of course. You're a special girl, Mimi. Seth

Broadhurst would be a lucky man to have a woman like you in his life. You can teach him how to relax."

Mimi swallowed. "Dad, Seth and I are not together. We…uh, we simply got stranded together on the way back from Hannah's wedding. The snowstorm and all, the roads were shut down—we had to stop and stay over."

Wiley's eyes narrowed. "You mean the two of you didn't…" He waved his fork in a vague gesture.

Mimi crossed her fingers beneath the table. She hated to lie to her dad, but how could she confess the truth? "No, Dad, of course not. Seth's a nice guy, and we danced and made the best of a rotten situation, but he's not my type." She faked a laugh for emphasis. "You know me, I want someone exciting. Not some boring, stodgy man in a suit who's glued to his pocket calendar. Why, he's not even that attractive."

"Then there was nothing between you. I mean, in the picture, it looked as if—"

"No way, Dad. Seth Broadhurst doesn't float my boat."

Her father cleared his throat, and Mimi turned and saw Seth standing behind her. He looked so handsome in his suit with snowflakes lingering in his hair that he nearly took her breath away.

But he wasn't smiling, she realized in horror. And from the hurt look on his face, he'd obviously overheard every word she'd said.

Chapter Seven

Seth put on his detached, unemotional face, the one he normally reserved for his patients, in a feeble attempt to pretend he hadn't overheard Mimi chop his self-esteem into tiny slivers like minced almonds.

Too late.

He saw the stunned look of regret that instantly clouded her bright blue eyes. "Seth, I'm—"

"It's nice to see you again, Mimi, Mr. Hartwell." Seth forced his gaze on Mimi's father, uncomfortable with the way Wiley squirmed and jumped up to pump his hand.

"Good to see you, too, Seth. Wish I could stay, but I gotta run. Business has been booming lately."

Mimi yanked at her father's arm. "Dad, don't..."

"Mr. Hartwell, please..."

Before either could finish, Wiley pecked Mimi on the cheek and bustled out, his white shoes clicking on the shiny black and white tiles of the coffee shop. Mimi stood, her hands clasped, her eyes wide and luminous. "Seth, I'm so sorry. I didn't mean—"

"You don't have to explain. I think you made yourself perfectly clear."

Mimi sighed. "You don't understand. Dad saw that picture in the newspaper and—"

"So did my parents." And he had defended her.

"Well, Alison saw it, too, and Dad got the wrong idea and thought we'd—" Mimi paused and lowered her voice to a whisper "—you know…slept together."

"We *did* sleep together."

"I know!" Mimi threw up her hands in exasperation. "But he really misinterpreted things and thought we were serious, as in a couple. Can you imagine that?"

No, he couldn't, could he?

"He's just so old-fashioned," she continued without waiting for his reply.

Maybe he was old-fashioned, too, Seth thought. *Boring and old-fashioned.*

"Before I could him tell how ridiculous the idea of us together was, he told me how great we'd be together—"

"Wiley said we'd be great together?"

"Yes. I had to do something or he'd have us married and settled down in no time. Neither of us want that."

"No, I can't imagine you ever settling down." Of course, according to her, he was already so settled he might as well have one foot in the grave. Besides, if Hannah had left him at the altar, Mimi would blast off in a cannon.

Mimi frowned and stacked the empty coffee cups together. "Since we'd agreed to keep that…er, that night a secret, I figured the best thing to do was make Dad see how wrong we'd be together.''

"I see."

She bit down on that plump little pink lip, reminding him of the way her mouth had tasted. "Really, Seth, we both know how different we are.''

"Right, I'm boring and stodgy.''

Mimi's expression softened. She obviously hadn't meant for him to overhear her comment. But that didn't mean she hadn't believed it. "Look, Seth, don't take it personally. We're simply wrong for each other and we both know it. You're a shrink, for heaven's sake, and I'm impulsive and emotional and I want to be an actress.'' She picked up the coffee cups and started toward the kitchen. He grabbed the dirty saucers and followed, well aware she'd said the word *shrink* as if it were a four-letter word.

"You don't have to carry dirty dishes,'' Mimi said.

"I don't mind. At least I can do something for you. Especially since I don't float your boat.''

Mimi put the cups in the sink, then turned to him, her hands on her hips. The movement drew her white blouse across her chest, accentuating every enticing curve and conjuring up images of her voluptuous body naked. "I'm sorry, I didn't mean to hurt your male pride.''

"So you were just acting last night?''

"No, well, yes, I mean, sure, you turned me on, but we were stranded and there was music and we were all alone.''

Great, he felt better now. "So if another man had

been around, you wouldn't have spent the night with *me?*''

''I didn't say that.''

''Yes, you did.''

''I did not. Stop putting words in my mouth.''

''I don't have to put words in your mouth. You seem to be doing fine on your own. In fact, you have quite the vocabulary.''

Mimi sighed and waved her hands. ''We both agreed we'd forget last night ever happened, that it was a mistake and we wouldn't repeat it, didn't we?''

''Yes.''

''So what are you doing here and why are you getting so defensive?''

He jammed his hands in the pockets of his ''boring'' suit, feeling edgy and out of sorts. He also had to think a minute to remember why he had come. Not to see her pretty face or hear that husky voice or touch her again.

No. None of those reasons.

''I came about work.''

A timer buzzed and Mimi grabbed a pot holder and opened the oven door. ''Let me check this new recipe and you can tell me what you want.''

Her. On top of that stainless-steel counter, naked and hot and writhing beneath him. He paused, stunned at his thoughts.

She pulled a muffin pan from the oven and placed it on the long worktable in the center of the big kitchen, oblivious to his fantasy. Pots and pans and mixing bowls filled the sink and counter. Cocoa and flour dotted the surface, and he heard the gritty sound of sugar grinding below his shoe. The mess didn't bother him as it normally would have because the delicious aroma of chocolate filled the air, reminding him of the hot fudge sundae she'd devoured at the Magnolia Manor and the way he'd licked the rich sauce from her lips.

He swallowed a groan and dug his hands deeper into his pockets. The weather outside was cold, but in the warm kitchen with Mimi he was burning up.

"Seth, are you going to explain why you're here?"

He tried to focus. "I'm starting a support group for single parents, and I'd like you to cater it."

Mimi began to frost a pan of brownies. "Is this a one-time deal?"

"No, we'll probably meet once a week for a while. I'm thinking Thursday evenings."

"How many people?"

He pulled out his notepad and saw her eyes flicker over the pad. "What?"

"I figured you carried one of those."

Right. She thought he was predictable, boring. He wasn't—he was simply responsible. What was wrong with that? "It helps with the job."

She nodded, looking unimpressed. "How many people?"

"Probably around ten adults the first time. Later on, I'd like to do some mixed groups, kids and parents, but the first meeting should be strictly adults."

"What do you want served? Hors d'oeuvres or just coffee and dessert?"

"Just coffee and dessert. Nothing fancy."

"Sounds doable. Why don't I bring something with strawberries and another dessert with chocolate."

The same two kinds of desserts they'd eaten in bed together. What was she trying to do, torture him?

"Seth?"

"No, how about fruitcake?"

"Fruitcake?"

He was thinking something with nuts since she was making him nutty. "I suppose not. I guess fruitcake is more of a Christmas dessert."

"I can try coconut, but really, strawberries and chocolate are much more popular."

"Fine."

She dropped a dollop of icing on her finger, lifted it and licked the thick frosting from the tip. His body surged with want, wicked fantasies bursting through his mind. Fantasies that Mimi Hartwell would not find boring at all.

Her gaze locked with his, heat flashing between them in a hot spiral. He brought his finger up and wiped the chocolate sauce from her cheek, then sucked his finger, savoring the delicious texture and taste of the frosting. He desperately wanted to taste Mimi again. Just one more time.

He had never felt desperate around a woman before. He didn't like the feeling.

Mimi's breath seemed to catch. "Seth..."

Hell, he didn't do desperate very well. "I know I don't float your boat," he said in a husky voice. He reached up to touch her. "And we're not right for each other."

Mimi licked her lips. "Seth, we...we can't."

He also knew she was right, but his heart had never pounded like this; his veins had never felt as if they had hot lust running through them with any other woman. Including Mimi's sister.

Hannah—one of the reasons they shouldn't be together.

All the other reasons collided in his head and he backed away, afraid if he didn't touch her, he'd shrivel up and become that boring, stodgy man she'd described. Even more afraid that if he did, he'd get burned. "I'll call about the meeting."

Mimi nodded. "I'll plan a menu."

He turned and left the kitchen, determined to maintain his distance. Determined to stay focused on his goals, on his job, on making a success of himself and living up to his family's expectations. On being rational, not desperate.

No matter how much it hurt him.

A WEEK LATER, Mimi circled the hope chest, her head swimming with worry, the nausea in her stomach rising to her throat. She could not be pregnant. No way, no how.

But Hannah's life had gone completely berserk when she'd received that heirloom ring, and inside her hope chest lay an antique baby rattle and a handmade baby quilt, and she had caught the bouquet, and she was late, and dear heavens…

She was so nervous she was babbling in her thoughts.

Mimi's hands shook as she reached for the home pregnancy test. She took a deep breath, opened the box and studied the directions. It might be a little early to take the test, but she had to do *something*. She was worrying herself into exhaustion. Seth had dropped by the coffee shop every day the past week, making her more nervous, asking about the menu for the support group and not asking about their relationship. Yet in a strange way he *was* asking—it was in his eyes. He was probably as desperate as she was to know they were safe from worry—he certainly hadn't been behaving in a friendly man-woman kind of way.

Not that she wanted him to.

Tears sprang to her eyes and she twisted the box in her hands. She was so emotional this week, too. All hormonal, which was a bad sign, too. Of course, it could be a good sign, a sign she was on the verge— why did women have to deal with all these hormones, anyway?

She almost dropped the box and had to spread the paper on top of the hope chest to read it. With every nerve in her body on alert, she removed the vial and headed for the bathroom. In a few minutes she would have the answer. She'd read the test results and feel better.

Then she could get on with her life, meet Hannah and Alison for lunch, and forget that she'd ever had any connection with Seth Broadhurst.

SETH STRUGGLED to maintain a professional expression as his parents sang the praises of the ER physician who'd replaced Hannah when she'd decided to go into family practice. Eleanor Bainbridge had graduated top in her class, completed a residency at Johns

Hopkins, had published several research papers and came with an impeccable reputation. He cut into his glazed chicken and forced himself to listen as she described her future goals—impressive.

"I'm delighted they've asked me to consider being head of ER. I've always wanted to settle in a small town."

"Sugar Hill General is lucky to have you on their staff," Seth's father said. "I say we have a toast."

Seth raised his glass dutifully and clinked his glass with everyone's, acknowledging the doctor's accomplishments with a sincere smile and giving his father a fake one. His parents were playing matchmaker. He had to admit Dr. Bainbridge was attractive. She had dark-blond hair, big brown eyes and a nice figure.

But she was the most boring woman he'd ever met.

Mimi would think he and Eleanor made the perfect couple.

"Seth has been on staff at Sugar Hill General for five years now," his mother said none too subtly. "I'm sure he wouldn't mind showing you around town, Dr. Bainbridge."

Seth shot her a warning look. She always thought she knew the type of woman best for him. Unfortunately none of them had ever floated his boat.

He ran a hand over his jaw, irritated. One night with Mimi and now he was starting to think like her. And he couldn't get her out of his mind. Mimi stirring chocolate frosting. Mimi in that short skirt with those dynamite legs. Mimi smiling up at him when they'd danced. Mimi lying naked in his arms.

Mimi, who didn't think he was all that attractive.

He was pathetic. All he could do was sit and compare her with every other woman he met.

Dr. Bainbridge pressed her hand over his. "I'd love to have you show me around, Seth—that is, if you don't mind."

Seth nodded, his jaw tight. Then his stomach twisted when he spotted Mimi and her sisters enter the restaurant.

THANK GOD the pregnancy test had been negative, Mimi thought when she spotted Seth having lunch with another woman. Not only having lunch but *holding hands.*

And in front of his parents. Someone they would approve of, no doubt.

Apparently he'd moved past his little fling with her and hadn't been too worried about the possibility of consequences from their night—not if he was already cozying up with someone else. Of course, his new girlfriend was probably a doctor like Hannah. Her stomach convulsed. Dear God, the woman even resembled Hannah. Maybe he still did have feelings for her sister.

"Oh, my gosh, there's Seth." Alison caught Mimi by the hand and gave her an odd look, then lowered her voice so Hannah wouldn't hear. "You want to go somewhere else?"

Mimi stopped in the entrance while Hannah spoke to the maître d'. "No, it's no big deal. We live in a small town. We're bound to run into each other all the time."

"Who's that woman with him?" Alison asked.

"She's the new head of ER." Hannah had returned, motioning that their table was ready. "I met her when they were conducting interviews."

Seth noticed them and waved. Mimi felt like flipping that hand backward and watching it slap him in the face.

She had no idea why. She and Seth were finished. Totally over. Especially now that she had the results of the pregnancy test.

"His parents still hate me," Hannah said.

Mimi saw the look his father and mother shot them and realized that part of their animosity was also directed toward her because of the picture in the newspaper. More guilt assaulted her. Of course, Hannah didn't know about the photograph.

"I'm glad I left the hospital." Hannah took a seat, oblivious to Mimi's discomfort. "It was just too weird."

As it would be if Hannah knew that Mimi had spent the night with Seth. Mimi trusted Alison and her father not to tell Hannah, but what about Seth's parents?

"His parents won't even speak to me," Hannah said.

Whew. Mimi breathed a sigh of relief. Thank goodness. Otherwise they might mention her.

"I wouldn't worry about Seth's folks," Alison said. "You did the right thing, Hannah. Seth knows that, too."

"Mrs. Broadhurst is such a society lady, and I embarrassed their son in public," Hannah said softly. "I guess you can't blame them for being upset."

Mimi shivered, her head suddenly feeling light as

she settled at the table. Unfortunately, although their table was on the opposite side of the room, she still had a clear view of Seth and his parents. What would the Broadhursts think if *she* turned up pregnant?

"That new doctor certainly is pretty," Mimi said, praying Hannah didn't hear the strain in her voice.

"Yes, she is." Hannah picked up her menu and scanned the entrées. "Maybe something will work out for her and Seth. I'm so happy with Jake I really want Seth to find the same kind of happiness."

"They look perfect for each other." Mimi wrinkled her nose as the waiter walked by with a steaming platter of clams. The strong odor sent her stomach into somersaults.

"Let's forget about Seth," Alison suggested. "We want to hear all about your honeymoon."

"And I want to hear about your date with that Ob-gyn," Hannah said to Alison. Hannah winked at Mimi. "I set her up with the guy that joined our practice last week."

"Sounds good to me," Mimi said. "I say we forget the whole Broadhurst family and focus on you two."

THIRTY MINUTES LATER though, Mimi hadn't been able to forget Seth. The mere sight of the food sitting on the table made her queasy, the task of swallowing the chicken she'd ordered impossible. Hannah had been chattering away about Jake and their wonderful honeymoon, but Mimi had barely been listening—she needed to focus all her effort on controlling the urge to throw up.

"Why don't we split a hot fudge cake?" Alison suggested.

The bright lights of the restaurant swirled in front of Mimi's eyes, black spots dancing. "I...excuse me." She jumped up, trotted to the bathroom, bumping into a waiter in her haste. He stumbled and lost his balance. The pot of coffee on his tray slid and landed in a fern by the mirrored wall. Mimi saw her pale reflection in the mirror, along with the curious stares of the diners. But she didn't dare stop to apologize for fear of embarrassing herself even more by losing her lunch in the plant.

Minutes later she sat hunched on the plush carpet of the ladies' room, her head between her knees, the room spinning, her mind a jumbled mess.

Hannah lay a cool, wet paper towel on the back of her neck. "Mimi, are you all right?"

Alison knelt beside her. "Sis, what's wrong?"

She squeezed her eyes shut in misery. "I don't know. Food poisoning, maybe."

"How long have you felt this way?" Hannah pressed her hand on Mimi's forehead.

"A few days." Mimi opened one eye and saw Alison's mouth form a worried *O*.

"Have you been running a fever?" Hannah asked.

"No."

"Diarrhea?"

"No."

"Just nausea?"

"And a little dizziness."

"Let's take you in for some tests. Maybe it's a weird strain of flu or something."

Mimi blinked back tears. "It has to be."

Hannah frowned and helped her stand. "You don't think you could possibly be pregnant, do you?"

Mimi and Alison exchanged worried looks.

"I...I don't think so. I did a test earlier, though."

Hannah sucked in a sharp breath. "And?"

"It was negative."

Hannah smiled. "That's good. Although those home tests aren't always reliable."

"They're not?"

Hannah shook her head. "No, honey. Sometimes if it's early, the tests can be wrong. And some of them are more sensitive than others."

Mimi gulped, clutching the wall for support.

Hannah patted her shoulder. "Don't worry. Ali and I are here."

"Yeah, we'll take care of you," Alison said softly.

Mimi felt even more miserable. She wanted to impress Hannah for a change, not be the little sister she had to rescue.

Oblivious to her turmoil, Hannah took charge in her big-sister way. "We'll take you to the clinic and run a blood test. Then we'll know for sure."

Alison squeezed her hand and Mimi bit down on her lip to stem the tears. "I can't be pregnant."

"Don't worry, sis," Hannah said. "We do the tests routinely. If you do have something treatable, I have to know before I can prescribe medication."

Mimi nodded. "All right, but I can't go out there like this."

"Don't be embarrassed." Alison curved an arm

around Mimi's waist for support. "Everyone gets sick, sis."

Mimi pulled away and brushed her hair from her face. "I'm feeling better now. Let me walk out on my own, okay?"

Hannah and Alison smiled in understanding. Mimi jutted her chin in the air, determined not to let Seth and his new lady friend see her as a weakling.

Chapter Eight

Seth's heart pounded in his chest as he left the restaurant. He had no idea if he'd been rude or had even said goodbye to his parents or the new ER doctor, but he'd mumbled an excuse and dashed from the table as soon as he'd seen the Hartwell sisters exit. Something was wrong with Mimi; her normally rosy cheeks were pale, and her vibrant eyes looked listless. His parents had glared at him, but he couldn't sit and feign interest in Dr. Bainbridge's long-winded description of her fossil collection when the woman who might be carrying his child was ill.

Odd how protective and afraid he felt for a woman he'd only spent one night with and a child that might not even exist.

He felt like a damn stalker as he wove in and out of traffic, lingering in the distance just far enough that Hannah, who was driving, wouldn't spot him. Several minutes later, when she braked in front of the Sugar Hill Family Clinic, his heart stopped. He parked across the street from the small building and slid down in his seat so he wouldn't be visible and watched Mimi climb out, wobbling as she walked up the steps. Alison and Hannah followed on each side like bodyguards, a reminder of the close relationship the three sisters shared. And how awkward it would be if his night with Mimi caused a rift between them.

Guilt and worry pressed against his lungs. Seth lay his head back and debated what to do. His first instinct, barbaric as it seemed, was to charge into the clinic and demand to know Mimi's condition.

He fought off the urge. His appearance would only make things worse. If she had something simple like the flu or a sinus infection or simply had bad cramps the way some women did, he'd look like a fool and would raise suspicions that would be hard to explain. Mimi wanted their night together to be kept a secret. And so did he.

At least, he had at first. Now he wasn't so sure.

He contemplated that strange realization for the next hour while patients came and went, his palms sweating as he gripped the steering wheel. A police car cruised by and he swore, sending a silent prayer that the cop didn't stop and question his presence. The policeman slowed and stared at him, and Seth straightened to his full height, grateful he'd worn his boring suit and tie. It didn't help. The cop parked and climbed out, patting his weapon as he strolled up to Seth's window. Seth wiped his damp palm on his pant leg and rolled down his window. "Hi, Officer."

"Hi. Mind telling me what you're doing parked at a yellow curb?"

Seth winced. "Sorry, sir. I didn't notice. I'll be glad to move."

The officer arched a brow. "Something going on?"

Seth opted for a white lie. "I drove a friend over to the clinic. Thought I'd wait out here and make a few calls while she saw the doctor." He gestured at his cell phone.

"Can I have your name, sir?"

"Dr. Seth Broadhurst. I'm a psychiatrist over at Sugar Hill General."

The officer crooked his hat sideways. "A shrink, huh?"

"Yes." Seth pulled out his business card and handed it to the man.

"Listen," the officer said, "I've been having trouble sleeping at night. Having these weird dreams."

Seth plastered on his professional face and tried to focus as the policeman sailed into a long diatribe about his odd dreams, mainly sexual in nature, which didn't sound all that odd.

"What do you think they mean?"

"You dream that you wake up naked and your wife has you handcuffed to the bed?"

"All the time. Then there's the one where I stop my wife's twin sister on the road for speeding, and…well, we do it in the back seat."

"Why don't you come by my office?" Seth suggested, not wanting to dispense advice on the street. "I have a friend who's an expert in analyzing dreams. Maybe you can talk to her."

"Great. I'll do that." The officer grinned and tipped his hat. "Have a good day."

I will, once I know Mimi's all right.

Seth moved his car to the other side of the street and watched the cop drive off, then turned back to stare at the clinic. What in blazes was taking so long? A quick check of his watch and he realized he had to be back at the hospital in twenty minutes. But he couldn't work until he talked to Mimi. And he wanted to do so in private.

He picked up his cell phone and called his secretary to reschedule his appointments—something he'd never done before. He told her he had a little emergency of his own. His heart squeezed painfully in his chest. If he didn't find out soon that Mimi was all right, he was going to have a coronary.

"YOU'RE PREGNANT," Hannah said.

Mimi glanced at Alison in panic. Alison glanced at Mimi in concern.

Mimi shook her head in denial. "I can't be."

"It's true, Mimi." Hannah gave her a sympathetic look. "The test is definitely positive."

"How far along?" Mimi asked.

Alison cradled her hand and squeezed it for support. Tears automatically blurred Mimi's vision.

"Just a few weeks." Hannah studied the chart for a moment. "Other than that, you're as healthy as can be. I can give you something for the nausea if it gets too bad, but you may want to try some soda crackers first."

Mimi nodded dumbly and Hannah sat on the exam table, letting her legs swing beside Mimi's. "It's going to be okay, Mimi. We'll take care of you."

"And we'll help you with the baby," Alison said softly.

"Ba...by." Mimi choked back a sob. "This all has to do with that hope chest Grammy gave me."

"What?" her sisters asked in unison.

Mimi explained about the baby blanket and rattle. Her sisters exchanged odd looks, then Hannah curved her arm around Mimi's shoulders. "Are you going to tell Joey?"

"Joey?" Mimi's blurred gaze swung to Alison's. Alison's eyes widened.

"Yeah, I know this must be difficult," Hannah said, "especially since he was arrested."

Mimi's pulse raced. Of course. Hannah would assume the baby was Joey's. "I...I suppose I should tell the father."

"You don't have to tell him right away," Hannah said. "Give yourself time to get used to the idea, sis. There's no rush. You have nine months."

Nine, long, tension-filled months.

Alison cleared her throat. "She doesn't *have* to tell Joey, does she? After all, he's in jail."

Hannah patted Mimi's hand. "Look, Mimi, it's up to you whether you tell Joey. For now, this will be our little secret."

Mimi nodded, knowing she should confess the truth to Hannah. She had never lied to her sister before, and she hated deceiving her now. There were too many secrets. But she couldn't tell her the truth...not yet. She couldn't bear the disappointment she'd see on Hannah's face.

And what about Seth? He'd told her that he didn't want kids. How could she tell him she was carrying his baby, especially when he was seeing someone else and when he still might be in love with Hannah?

THREE HOURS LATER, Seth stood on Mimi's porch, his knees knocking as he waited for her to answer the doorbell. He'd driven by a dozen times in the past few hours and seen Hannah's car in the drive, so he'd waited. With every passing second, his imagination had gotten wilder. He told himself Mimi's condition couldn't be serious or Hannah would have taken her to the hospital. But his fears had escalated until he'd almost developed a nervous twitch.

Mimi was pregnant and needed help. Mimi would never even tell him. Dear God, Mimi had had a miscarriage.

He ran a hand over his face, grateful Hannah and Alison had finally left. He'd never sleep tonight unless he saw for himself that Mimi was all right.

He finally heard feet shuffling inside and Mimi's voice. "Who's there?"

"It's me. Seth."

"Seth?" Her voice squeaked, alarming him more.

"I have to see you for a minute. Please let me in."

"Seth, I…I'm really tired. Can't it wait until tomorrow?"

He considered making up a phony excuse, but exhaustion clouded his brain and his patience snapped. "No. Now either open the damn door or I'm going to break it down."

"What?"

"Please. I have to see you." He hated the desperation in his voice.

Mimi slid back the lock and opened the door. Her pale face poked through the tiny opening, and his heart thundered at the sight of her swollen red-rimmed eyes.

"Take off the damn chain and let me in."

"Seth, what in the world's wrong? You sound upset."

He took a deep breath. She was right. He didn't sound like himself. Worry did that to a man, tore him inside out and made him crazy. "I'm sorry. I'm not angry, just concerned. I really want to come in."

She bit down on her lip, her chin trembling.

"Mimi, please. I promise I won't stay long."

She sighed and closed her eyes as if trying to decide, but finally disengaged the chain. He tried to calm himself as he walked inside, stepping by a laundry basket in the foyer. Colorful, odd-shaped contemporary furniture filled her small apartment. A bright yellow U-shaped sofa, purple swivel chair, beanbags chairs covered in a leopard-skin print. Magazines and books were scattered on the coffee table, a pile of shoes tossed in the corner beside a rubber chew toy that had been mangled by an animal. He shuddered, unable to help comparing her home with his tidy, well-kept one. Mimi obviously didn't have a cleaning compulsion.

A Chinese pug lay snoring on a lime-green shag rug, and a gray cat was curled up on the sofa—probably the mangler of the chew toy. The minute Seth stepped into the room, the dog leaped up, snarled and dove for his leg.

Seth had never been around animals much. He

jumped backward and tried to shake the dog loose, but the little animal latched onto his pant leg, sinking his teeth in deeper as if he wanted to take a bite out of Seth.

"Good grief, call him off, Mimi, before he kills me."

"He won't kill you." Mimi stooped and reached for the animal, her voice a soft purr. "Come here, Wrangler. What's wrong with you, bud?" She eased the dog away from Seth, taking a chunk of his gray slacks with her, then calmed the dog while Seth stood shaking, wondering about the status of the dog's rabies shots.

"I'm sorry. I'll replace the pants." Mimi stared at him in confusion. "He's usually so friendly. I don't know what set him off."

The dog narrowed his beady eyes. Seth stiffened.

"You don't like animals?" Mimi asked.

"It's not that I don't like them."

"But you're not comfortable with them, are you?"

Seth hesitated, wondering why her question sounded like an accusation. "Not really. My parents never allowed pets. Mother thought them barbaric and dangerous."

She nodded. "Figures."

"What does that mean?"

"First, animals can sense if someone doesn't like them. And second, your parents don't look like pet people." She gestured around the den. "On the other hand, I can't imagine living without a pet or two. Or three."

He remembered Hannah saying that Mimi did some

volunteer work with the Humane Society, that sometimes she acted as a foster parent for injured or stray animals until the society could find them homes. But he didn't want to talk about her pets.

He wanted to talk about her. To hold her.

She hugged a fuchsia robe around herself and gestured toward one of the chairs, then sat down on the sofa and stroked the pug's back as he curled in her lap. She avoided Seth's gaze. "Do you want some coffee or tea?"

"No. I want to know if you're okay."

His voice shook and she glanced at his face, her expression wary. "I'm fine. Why wouldn't I be?"

"When you left the restaurant earlier, you looked ill."

Her pouty mouth tried to form a smile, but it appeared weak, and her hands trembled as she pushed a strand of that long wild hair behind her ear. "I'm fine."

"The hell you are." He stood, his hands fisted on his hips. "I saw you at the clinic. Now tell me the truth. Are you all right?"

Her eyes widened. "You followed me to the clinic?"

He hesitated. He hadn't meant to tell her that tidbit. "Yes. I was worried."

"Well, you have no reason to worry," she said as if he had no *right* to worry, which only made him angrier. "My sisters took care of me. Besides, why would you leave your lunch date on account of me?"

"Leave my lunch date? I not only left, I sat outside the clinic like a damn stalker and almost got ar-

rested.'' He began to pace. ''Then I lied to my secretary, canceled my appointments for the day, something I've never done before, and drove by your place
waiting for your sisters to leave. Then I sat outside
for another hour trying to figure out why you hadn't
called *me* if you weren't feeling well.''

Mimi seemed surprised by his speech. She thrust
out that little chin. ''Why would I call *you?* We're
not even dating, Seth.''

He was surprised, too. He never lost control. At
least he never had before he met Mimi. Besides, she
did have a point.

''I'm sorry, Seth. Nobody asked you to follow me
or cancel your appointments. I don't understand why
you'd drive by or make such a big deal—''

''Because I thought you might be pregnant!''

She snapped her lips together, then opened them to
ask, ''Why would you think that?''

''Because we were together and you looked ill and
I started thinking and putting two and two together—''

''I had food poisoning,'' Mimi said in a low voice.

Her words stopped him in his tracks. All afternoon
he'd been preparing himself to learn he was going to
be a father. He wasn't sure whether to be relieved
or…a little disappointed. ''Food poisoning?''

''Yes.''

He sank onto the sofa and exhaled, emotions churn-
ing through him. Relief. Frustration. Tension. Worry
that she still might not be telling him the truth.

He felt like a fool.

She pulled at a loose thread on her robe. "It hit me really quickly in the restaurant, but Hannah says food poisoning does that. Comes out of nowhere and knocks you for a loop. She took me to the clinic and fixed me up, but it has to run its course…" She finally stopped as if she realized she was babbling.

"So, you've been feeling okay otherwise? Before today at lunch?"

"Yes."

"No morning sickness?"

"Really, Seth." Mimi shook her head and stood. "You're worrying for nothing. I just got sick on that glazed chicken. My stomach's already settling."

"You don't need anything, then?"

"No. I'll be fine tomorrow. I simply need to rest."

She did look exhausted.

"I suppose I should go, let you get some sleep."

She nodded and walked him to the door, but his legs still felt shaky.

He studied her ashen skin, the almost purple bruises beneath her eyes, the way her chin quivered, and he wanted to reach out and hold her so badly he ached. But she'd been ill and, as she pointed out, she had her sisters. The two of them weren't a couple. They never would be.

She didn't even find him that attractive.

Her words haunted him all the way home. When he finally crawled into bed, he remembered she'd said she'd gotten food poisoning from the chicken. He bolted up in bed, his pulse racing. He'd eaten the chicken, too, and *he* hadn't gotten sick.

MIMI LAY IN THE DARKNESS of her bedroom, staring at the ceiling, replaying the day's events, tears dribbling down her cheeks. She should have told Hannah the truth. And Seth. She would have to eventually. Only she didn't have the energy now, not so soon after learning the news herself. Besides, Hannah had just returned from her honeymoon. If she knew the truth, she would worry, would try to be the caretaker, just as she always did. Mimi had been trying so hard to be independent, to prove she could stand on her own two feet, even if they were klutzy and too big for her height.

She lay her hand across her stomach and envisioned the changes that would take place over the next few months. The obvious physical changes. The mental and emotional ones. The changes in her career plans. There was so much to think about, so many adjustments.

A baby. A real live little person who would depend on her. Who needed her.

Her baby would need a daddy, too.

Just like she and her sisters had needed their father.

On the other hand, she and her sisters had gotten along fine with just one parent.

Not that they hadn't missed having a mother around...

She closed her eyes and hiccuped on a sob. She didn't want to disappoint her family, not her father or Hannah or Alison. And she didn't want to disappoint Seth. To make him feel trapped. Tied to a woman he didn't want. Saddled with a child he'd had with the wrong woman.

After seeing him with that other doctor today, she knew she'd never fit into his world. Just the sight of his parents made her legs shake and rattle. And look at the way her dog had reacted to him and the way he'd reacted to Wrangler. She massaged her stomach, tears overflowing.

No, she and Seth were completely wrong for each other.

Chapter Nine

Seth buried himself in work the next week and staunchly avoided Mimi. He couldn't believe what a fool he'd been, barging in and demanding she talk to him. Especially after the things she'd said about him to her father.

But all week reminders of Mimi jumped out at him, grinding his nose in the memory of that one wild night together. Her scent lingered in his car as if the leather seats had absorbed her potent perfume permanently. And apparently Mimi, or her father, had devised an advertising stunt to boost business at her café. He'd seen a white customized van cruising the streets sporting a huge chocolate cake twirling on top, red streaks representing raspberry sauce running down the sides, an intercom blasting an invitation to visit the Sugar Hill Café.

He hadn't gone near the place.

But today he was going to see her anyway.

He adjusted his burgundy tie and combed his hair, reminding himself his evening would be spent leading the first support group for single parents, not enjoying a date with Mimi. But after four days without seeing her he... He'd what? He was going crazy?

How could that possibly be when he knew as well as she did how ill-suited they were? He was simply worried about her health. Once he knew for certain their erotic night hadn't resulted in a pregnancy, he could rest easily and extricate her from his mind.

A few minutes later he hurried to greet Mimi at the community center, but when he arrived, she'd already arranged the tables.

He walked up behind her, admiring the view as she set out the refreshments. "Hi. It looks like you have things under control."

Mimi jumped and spun around, her eyes big and sparkling. "Hi. Yes, I think we're all set."

"The food looks great." He gestured toward the strawberry shortcake and the mudslinger chocolate pie. She'd also brought a tray filled with a mixture of cookies and a coffee cake that smelled of cinnamon and apples. "My stomach's rumbling already."

"The coffee should be ready soon. I also made a fruit punch and brought sodas."

"You thought of everything."

She nodded. He had slept with this woman, had seen and touched and tasted every delicious inch of her. Yet now they'd resorted to chitchat.

He started to comment, but the room suddenly filled with parents. Relief flooded Mimi's eyes, and he vowed to corner her later and find out if she'd suffered from any more bouts of food poisoning.

MIMI WATCHED SETH mingle with the group of single parents, introducing the various attendees, his large hands moving as he spoke, his deep voice titillating.

Just the way it had been when he'd called her name in the throes of passion.

Darn it, why couldn't she go back to seeing him the way she had before? As boring old Seth, the shrink, not sexy Seth, the man who'd made love to her so tenderly she'd nearly wept. Seth, the father of her baby.

The man she wanted to hold her all night long.

Her hand automatically covered her still-flat stomach, and she swallowed, wishing she could gain the courage to tell him. And Hannah and her father. But so far, she'd barely been able to accept the news herself.

She sliced the chocolate cake, her stomach twisting again as it did so often these days, her hand trembling as she fought the nausea. She'd opted for no medicine, concerned that it might affect the baby, but if her queasy stomach didn't settle soon, she'd be forced to contact Hannah. She couldn't continue existing on crackers. It couldn't be good for her—or the baby.

Mimi took her place behind the table to serve while everyone lined up for refreshments. Her stomach roiled again, her nerves teaming up with her condition, making things worse. She fought off the feeling, grateful when the last person accepted a plate.

"I know it's hard on Wilfred to be without his father," one of the mothers said. "But what can I do? He ran off three months ago and I don't have a clue where he is."

"My boyfriend skipped out the minute I told him

I was pregnant," another young woman commented. "The big chicken didn't want the responsibility."

Mimi stood on the periphery of the group, tempted to join in. To ask them about single parenting. Yet she couldn't, not with Seth watching.

"I'm glad my old man's not around," a tall lady wearing a hot-pink suit said. "He drinks so much he'd be a bad influence on my kids."

But Seth would be a good influence. He'd make a great father, especially if he loosened up a bit.

"My wife is the worst mother," a slender man who looked to be in his thirties complained. "She's too busy with her job for the kids. That's the reason I divorced her."

"Do they live with her?"

"We're in the middle of a custody battle now."

Mimi lapsed into thought as she set out the coffee condiments. She would have to make a decision about her career—would she be able to pursue acting now or should she get a real job, something steadier than managing the café? Her own mother had callously deserted her and her sisters to pursue her own dreams. Could Mimi do the same?

No. But if she didn't pursue acting, what else could she do? Go back to school?

Memories of her childhood floated back. When their mother left, Wiley had picked up the pieces and raised them by himself. Their dad had been the world to them. Could she deny her own baby its father?

But your baby won't be like you—it'll have a mother, she argued silently.

Even if you land the part on that soap, if your acting career takes off, what will you do with an infant while you travel?

Seth's voice jarred her from her troubled thoughts. "Listen, folks, why don't we all sit down."

Everyone obeyed, hushed murmurs filtering around the room. Seth began the session with a discussion of common problems single parents faced. "Several of you have said that you feel alone. I thought it would be good for you to meet and offer support to one another. I suggest you use this time to form friendships, maybe you can even trade advice, what's working and not working, discuss day-care issues."

The session seemed to be successful, enthusiasm growing as the individuals shared. Mimi watched with a mixture of admiration and trepidation. Her respect for Seth's professionalism grew, her earlier skepticism about him being a shrink dissipating as she realized the importance of his work. Her respect for her father also rose, while her own insecurities over parenting escalated. Would she sit in a group like this someday, asking strangers for parenting advice because of her single-parent status?

The mere thought sent a sick feeling climbing up her throat. Several people had discarded their dirty plates in the trash, and the smells of chocolate frosting, strawberries and pineapple punch only added to the nausea. It hit her fast and unrelentlessly. She covered her mouth and raced from the room, praying she'd make it to the ladies' room in time. She only hoped Seth hadn't seen her.

SETH ENDED the session and said goodbye to his patients as quickly as humanly possible, but Mrs. Flat and her husband, Ralph, had lingered. He'd realized the two of them had some issues, along with an underlying affection for each other, so he'd spent an extra few minutes setting up a couples' session with them. They just might salvage their marriage yet, if both of them could simply let go of their stubborn pride. He'd certainly forgotten his own pride tonight and had found himself constantly looking at Mimi.

Now he was worried about her. He'd seen her beautiful smile fade and her rosy cheeks grow pale, no *green,* and his own stomach had convulsed. She'd disappeared over half an hour before. He was damned tired of waiting for her.

He stalked to the ladies' room, listened at the door, heard silence and knocked gently. No reply.

She had to be in there. She still had her catering supplies to collect. He knocked again and thought he heard a faint voice, so he pushed the door open. "Mimi?"

"Seth?"

"Yeah. Are you all right?"

"Go away."

Her weak voice sent alarm shooting up his spine. He slowly eased himself in the sitting area, not wanting to intrude on her privacy, yet desperate to know she was okay. "Mimi, where are you?"

A sniffle sounded from the washroom connected to the vanity area. "I said go away."

"I'm not leaving until you come out."

"I can't come out right now," she said in a miserable voice.

"Why not?"

"I... Just go away. I'll be out in a few minutes."

"No."

"Seth, please leave."

Obviously she meant the statement as a warning, but her voice sounded weak, as if she needed help. He slowly moved through the opening that served as a doorway from the sitting room to the washroom section and spotted Mimi's black heels peeking from the last stall. She was sitting on the floor, her legs tucked beneath her. Alarm bells clanged in his head again, and he pushed open the door.

"Seth, please..."

She had one arm draped over the toilet seat, her head drooping pathetically, her face a ghostly white. His heart clutched and he capitulated into motion. Seconds later, he returned with a cool wet cloth and pressed it to her neck, then gently wiped her face and forehead.

"Seth, please just go..."

"Shh." He pressed the cloth to her forehead. She murmured thanks in a weak voice.

"Food poisoning again, huh?"

Her whole body stiffened. With a pitiful sigh, she dropped her head over her arms again as if to avoid answering him. Worry and fear and...a little trickle of something that felt like excitement, seeped into him. He knew the answer. Somehow he'd known all along.

"Are you going to be sick again? Should I call a doctor?"

She shook her head.

"You're sure?"

She nodded.

"All right. Then I'm going to lift you and take you to the sofa in the sitting area."

She sniffled again and he realized she was crying, so he slid his arms beneath her and lifted her against his chest. She turned her head into him, draping one limp arm around his neck and whispering something that sounded like a protest. The misery in her face tore at him. He took charge, determined to care for her no matter how much she protested.

He gently lay her on the velvety cushions and propped her head on a pillow. Her hair had escaped the pins she'd used to secure it and curled around her face, making her look young and vulnerable. He wanted to hold her and promise her everything would be all right. But the memory of her conversation with her father still haunted him.

"Do you want me to get Hannah?"

She shook her head and looked at him. Her eyes were big, luminous, filled with tears and worry and regret. "I'm s-sorry."

He smiled and brushed a strand of hair from her forehead. "For what?"

"For—" she gestured toward her prone state "—for this."

His throat grew thick. "You don't have to apologize for being sick." For God's sake, she'd gotten sick because she was carrying his baby.

She bit down on her lip and stared at the ceiling tiles as if she might see an answer written there. He rubbed her chin with his thumb and turned her face to his, forcing her to look at him. "When were you going to tell me?"

Her mouth tightened.

"Were you ever?"

"I..."

"Don't lie to me again, Mimi."

His voice sounded harsher than he'd intended, and he started to apologize when she spoke up. "Hannah thinks the...baby is Joey's."

The air whooshed from his lungs. "She what?"

"I did a test and it was negative, but then I got sick, and Hannah insisted on doing the test, and I couldn't think of a way out of it, and she told me the test was positive, and she assumed—"

"That the baby, *our* baby, belongs to Joey?"

She nodded.

"And you didn't correct her?"

Her eyes turned grave. "No, I didn't think...you'd want her to know."

"You mean *you* didn't want her to know you'd been with me." Hurt, however irrational, welled in his chest.

She shook her head, her chin quivering. A lone tear spilled down her cheek. "I didn't want it to be true."

Her words cut right through him. She didn't want to have his baby. Of course she wouldn't—she didn't even think he was all that attractive. Why would she want to be tied to him or have his child? Probably afraid she'd have some boring, stodgy little boy who resembled him...

He stood and turned away from her, his spine stiff, afraid if she saw his face, she'd read the emotion in his eyes, emotion he'd never felt before and certainly didn't know how to deal with now.

Mimi saw Seth turn away and knew he was hiding his feelings. He was angry with her for not telling him the truth. Was he angry she'd gotten pregnant? Angry he'd be tied to her because of a child he didn't want?

"Seth, I know you didn't want kids. And I…I don't expect anything from you."

He whirled around. "You don't expect anything?"

"No. I mean, I'd never try to trap you—"

"You're having my child. Whether you like it or not, Mimi, that baby connects us."

She heard the bitterness in his voice, and a fresh ache seized her. "But it doesn't have to. You don't have to be involved."

"You think I'd shirk my responsibilities, that I'm the kind of man who'd run out on his child like husbands and boyfriends of the women who were here tonight."

No, she didn't. Seth would assume responsibility— he was that kind of man. But she wanted more out of a relationship. Not that he was offering one; he might simply be referring to child support. "I know you're responsible, Seth. I just don't want you thinking I trapped you. That's what happened to my parents, and look how it turned out."

"What are you talking about?"

"My mom and dad. They only got married because Mom was pregnant with Hannah." Good grief, she realized in horror. Seth had never mentioned marriage. She certainly didn't want him to think *she* wanted it. Besides, Hannah had been with Seth first—another reminder of the reason they shouldn't be in this situation.

His eyes darkened. "Hannah never told me. But you're right, we should get married."

"No, I wasn't suggesting marriage!" She struggled to sit up, but Seth gently eased her back down.

"Listen, Mimi, we're two decent people here. We're both fairly responsible and care about the future of this child. It's the right thing to do."

"It would never work."

"We can make it work."

"No, we can't."

How can you be so sure?"

"I overheard Mom and Dad arguing the day Mom left. She said she only married Dad because of the pregnancy. They were too different and they ended up hating each other."

Seth fisted his hands by his sides. "So you think we'll end up hating each other?"

"I don't know. Yes. No. Probably." Mimi took a deep breath. Fortunately the worst of the nausea had subsided. She felt weak, but better. "I don't want you feeling some misguided sense of responsibility. I can take care of myself."

His gaze slid over her. "Yeah, you're doing a great job."

Mimi hissed. "I'll be fine."

"What about the baby?"

She pushed herself to a sitting position, grateful the room had finally stopped spinning. "I'll take care of him, too."

His eyebrow arched. "It's a boy?"

"I don't know. That was just a figure of speech." Had his voice actually sounded wistful? "It's too early to tell."

He nodded and she stood, brushing away his hands when he tried to help her. "I...I should go clean up."

"I'll clean up the damn dishes. You are going to rest."

She struggled for a calming breath. "Seth, I'm okay now. I intend to do my job."

"I said I'll clean up. You can sit in the chair and watch." He folded his arms across his chest, towering over her, looking impossibly masculine and tough, especially for a boring shrink. Only, she had trouble seeing the boring part now. He was hot and rough-looking, emotion adding color to his cheeks, his square jaw set firmly, his eyes flashing anger and turmoil. And God help her she wanted him again. Just once more, wild and hot, right here on the sofa in the ladies' room.

She must be sick again—no, she was a *sicko*. A pathetic pregnant hormonal sicko.

"I don't like orders, Seth."

A muscle ticked above his eyebrow. "And I don't like the fact that Hannah thinks my baby belongs to some criminal."

Mimi's heart capitulated briefly at his possessive tone—he almost sounded as if he wanted the baby. But she must be fooling herself. He'd made himself clear the night they'd talked; he simply felt responsible now. She'd injured his male pride. And if he cared so much about what Hannah thought, he must still have feelings for her....

Chapter Ten

Seth contemplated what to do while he cleaned up. Unfortunately no earth-shattering revelations hit him. He insisted on following Mimi back to her house, his mind still grasping for answers as he parked behind her on the drive. Here he was, with a 130 IQ, a doctorate in psychology, a man who counseled people with all kinds of disorders and situations, ranging from complex schizophrenia to single parenthood, but he had no idea how to handle his own problem.

Not that the baby was a problem. He would never think of his own child as anything but a little miracle. But this strained relationship with Mimi was another story. Part of him wanted to throw her down and make love to her again until she admitted how perfectly they complemented each other, which unfortunately he still didn't know if he believed, while part of him wanted to hold her gently and promise her everything would be all right.

But how could it be when she didn't want him around? When she was so upset over the pregnancy and so against Hannah knowing and so *not attracted* to him?

HE FOLLOWED Mimi up the steps, juggling the box of leftover paper products and the coffeepot.

"Thanks, Seth, but you didn't have to follow me home."

"I didn't mind." He considered asking Mimi if he could come in and talk when he heard another car drive up.

Mimi groaned and threw a frustrated look over her shoulder. "It's Hannah and Alison."

"You want me to get rid of them?"

"Of course not." Mimi unlocked the door and pushed inside while her sisters climbed from Hannah's Volvo. "But I know they've come to check on me like little mother hens."

"They care about you," Seth said, shifting the box so he could set it down as he followed her inside. "And so do I."

"Seth, don't."

"Don't what?"

Mimi's eyes trapped him with a pleading look. "Don't say things like that. I know you feel responsible, but—"

"But—"

"Hey, Mimi." Hannah poked her head through the opened door, confusion registering on her face when she spotted Seth in the foyer. "I thought that was your car."

"Come on in," Mimi said in a cheery voice. "Seth was just leaving."

Seth stiffened. She obviously wanted to get rid of him.

Wrangler ran up and barked at him, and Mimi knelt

to calm the pug while Alison bustled in. An odd sparkle lit her eyes when she saw him, and he wondered if she knew about his night with Mimi. "Hi, Seth."

"He helped me bring things back from the support group," Mimi quickly explained.

"What kind of support group?" Alison asked.

"It's for single parents," Mimi said.

Hannah arched a brow while a sly grin tugged at Alison's face.

"I catered it for him," Mimi said, apparently not wanting them to know that Seth knew about the baby.

Hannah grinned at him. "Sounds like a great program, Seth. I hope it's successful."

"If tonight's any indication, I think it will be," Seth said.

Alison held up a grocery bag. "We brought ice cream. Mint chocolate chip."

Mimi smiled weakly. "Great. Go get three spoons."

Seth frowned, said good-night and left. It didn't take a genius to realize she didn't want to discuss her pregnancy in front of him. Hurt once more suffused him. She'd rather her sisters believe Joey had fathered her baby.

A few minutes later, Mimi curled on the couch in her terry-cloth robe, eating ice cream from the carton with her sisters just as they'd done when they were little girls.

"I'm starting the renovations for the bridal shop," Alison said.

"Cool." Mimi dug into the carton. "We need some more businesses downtown."

"Let me know if I can help, sis," Hannah said.

Alison took the carton from Mimi and picked a chocolate chip from it, popping it into her mouth. "Thanks, but I have things under control for now."

"So how are you feeling, Mimi?" Hannah asked.

Mimi licked her spoon and confided about her earlier bout of nausea.

"That does it. I'm writing you a prescription."

"I won't take anything that might hurt the baby."

Hannah smiled and patted her back. "This is safe, sis, trust me. We give it to a lot of pregnant women."

"I still can't believe I'm pregnant," Mimi said, her spoon in midair. "I...feel like such a mess-up."

Hannah and Alison traded sympathetic looks. "You used birth control?" Hannah asked.

Mimi nodded. "Well, I...we forgot once."

"That's all it takes," Hannah said dryly.

"Uh-oh. I heard this lecture when I was twelve," Alison said. "Mother Hannah."

The girls laughed in unison. "I guess I was bossy," Hannah admitted.

Mimi squeezed Hannah's hand. "When Mom left, you obviously felt responsible because you were the oldest. I'm sorry I wasn't more help."

"I never minded," Hannah said softly. "And I'm here for you now, Mimi."

Mimi's eyes filled with tears. "I know. But I don't want you to keep cleaning up my mistakes. I'm a big girl now. I can take care of myself."

Hannah smoothed a strand of hair from Mimi's cheek. "That's ridiculous. I love you. I don't mind helping you. Besides, I've always admired you, Mimi.

You're creative and fun and you have so much spunk. I wish I was more like you.''

"What?''

"It's true,'' Hannah said. "You have a lot going for you, sis. This baby's lucky to have a loving, caring, talented mom like you. And I promise to babysit if you get that part on the soap.''

"Me, too.'' Alison stretched her jean-clad legs in front of her. "Hannah's right. You'll make a great Mom.''

Mimi took the compliment to heart, perking up at the reminder of the soap opera. Tomorrow after work she'd rehearse the belly-dancing routine.

Hannah frowned and once again dug into the carton of ice cream with her spoon. "Have you decided if you're going to tell Joey?''

Mimi glanced at Alison's raised eyebrows. What should she do? Confess the truth to Hannah? Chance her relationship with her sister for her nonrelationship with Hannah's old boyfriend? For the best sex…man she'd ever been with?

"Mimi?'' Hannah sounded worried.

"No, I'm not going to tell Joey.''

Because he's not the father. She tried to say the words out loud, but they refused to push past her lips.

"How about…''

Mimi narrowed her eyes at Alison, afraid she intended to spill the truth.

"How about Dad?'' Alison asked. "And Mom?''

Mimi frowned. "I'll have to tell Dad sometime, but I don't know about Mom. Besides, she hasn't stopped by to see me since she moved back.''

Alison spooned up another bite of ice cream. "Dad said she went back to L.A. to tie up her affairs before the move."

"Affairs?" Hannah asked.

"Does Mom have another man in her life now?" Mimi asked.

Alison shrugged. "I don't know. I assumed he meant her business. She put her condo on the market. She'll be back any day." She paused, angling her head in thought. "I wonder what it'll be like with her living in Sugar Hill."

"Awkward," Hannah said quietly.

"Definitely awkward," Mimi agreed. Just as it would be when everyone found out Seth, not Joey, was the father of her baby.

"HERE, I BROUGHT YOU breakfast." Seth placed a paper bag on the counter of the coffee shop and grinned at Mimi.

Mimi simply stared at him. "Why?"

"Because breakfast is the most important meal of the day, and I wasn't sure you ate it." One of the many things they didn't know about each other. But he was determined to rectify that situation. After all, two people who'd made a baby together should know a few things about each other. He had nine months to do his homework.

Mimi shook her head. "Have you forgotten that I work at a café?"

"You sell desserts, not nutritious meals. And you need to eat a regular, balanced diet now—"

"Shh." Mimi put her finger over his lips for emphasis. He couldn't help but smile at her touch. Warmth seeped into him, generating enough heat to set him on fire. But Seth ignored his clamoring libido and pulled out a container of grits, a plate of eggs, bacon and toast.

"We serve bagels and fruit and muffins in the morning, and soup and salads for lunch." Mimi frowned at the huge breakfast. "Besides, I couldn't possibly eat all that."

He reached for her hand, concerned. "You aren't sick again this morning, are you?"

Mimi pulled away. "No, Hannah gave me something for the nausea, but I ate already."

He raised a brow in question. "And?"

"I can take care of myself, Seth."

"So I keep hearing." Seth leaned a hip against the bar stool, wondering how she could look so sexy and sweet at the same time. Her skin was rosy this morning, her eyes perky, her body voluptuous in her little black skirt and white blouse. One of the top buttons had slipped though its casing, giving him a glimpse of soft, inviting flesh. He knew what lay below…

"Look, I have work to do, Seth. So why don't you run on to your big office and analyze someone?"

He placed a book on the counter. "I don't have an appointment until ten. Thought I'd stop by and have a cup of coffee and read a little."

Her gaze fell to his book, *A Hundred Questions about Pregnancy,* and she rolled her eyes. "Put that away."

He opened it. "I've gathered all kinds of information on pregnancy and raising kids. I thought I'd study the material while you eat your breakfast.''

''I'm not eating all that cholesterol and fat.''

''All right. Next time I'll bring fresh fruit and—''

''There won't be a next time, Seth.'' She snapped his book shut. ''And I told you to put that thing away.''

''I'm simply trying to understand you and your...condition. We could read the book together.''

The door swung open and two businessmen strode in. Mimi moved away to wait on them, but the young girl who worked for her handled the order, forcing her to remain with him.

''It says here pregnant women are emotional—''

''I'm always emotional.''

''And moody.''

''That, too.''

''They have food cravings. Are you craving anything?''

She glared at him. ''Peace and quiet.''

He nodded. ''Sometimes they don't sleep well. Especially in the later months when—''

''When they get big and fat and unattractive.''

''I don't think pregnant woman are unattractive.'' Seth accepted the cup of coffee, studying her. ''And I hate skinny women.''

Mimi shrugged. ''I really don't want to talk about this with you, Seth.''

''So who are you going to talk about it with? Your father? Alison and Hannah?''

She refilled the sugar container as if she needed

something to do, spilling sugar over the sides. "I don't know."

"I'm a good listener, Mimi."

"You're a shrink. You get paid to listen."

"You can lie on my couch for free."

He didn't try to hide the suggestive tone in his voice. He'd dreamed about Mimi last night and he felt wicked this morning, unable to keep himself from teasing her. In his dream she'd been lying in his bed, naked and warm, curled in his arms, her hair tickling his chest, her hand... The dream had been so erotic he'd thought it was real. He'd felt her soft skin, tasted her delicious mouth, rubbed his hand over the soft roundness of her belly where his baby lay.

He leaned closer. "I'm going to be a part of this baby's life, too. You might as well get used to it."

The bell above the door jingled again. Mimi's face clouded. He pivoted to see what had upset her and saw her father enter the café, a slender, sophisticated-looking woman beside him. Mimi's mother.

No wonder Mimi seemed upset.

"Have you told Wiley yet?" he asked in a low voice.

She slid Seth a warning look. "No, not yet. And don't start psychoanalyzing me about it, either."

His heart squeezed at her confused tone. "I'm trying to make this easier on you, Mimi. Just tell me how to help."

Mimi frowned at her parents, then swung her gaze back to him. "You can give me some space. I need to be alone for a while."

He felt as if she'd kicked him in the gut, but he

nodded, picked up his book and coffee and walked out the door. He'd give her exactly what she'd asked for, but he didn't like it one damn bit.

MIMI WATCHED HIM leave, guilt tugging at her. She was not a cruel person, had never hurt anyone in her life, yet she realized she had just hurt Seth. He'd been sweet and sexy and wonderfully nice to her, and she'd thwarted his every attempt at friendship. Why, she didn't know. Well, maybe she did know—he was only being nice to her because of the baby. She didn't want all that…kindness—she wanted the real thing. She wanted him to be attracted to Mimi, the woman, not Mimi who'd gotten pregnant with his child.

Yes, she admitted silently, she wanted him to be attracted to her because, different or not, stodgy, boring shrink or not, Seth was the nicest, most tender, understanding, kindest, sexiest man she'd ever met.

Darn it. She could not fall for her baby's father.

Even if Seth did find her attractive and was interested in her for some reason other than the baby, which she didn't believe for a minute, he'd grow tired of her when he realized she didn't fit into his world. He'd walk away. And she would be left with a broken heart.

As if to cement her thoughts, her parents entered the café and headed straight toward her, looking tense and anxious—a definite reminder of the catastrophic ending to a forced marriage.

"How's my girl doing?" Mimi's father threw his arms around her. "I've been missing you."

"I'm fine, Daddy. It's good to see you, too." Mimi

hugged him back and gestured toward her mother, who stood on the opposite side of the counter, looking uncomfortable and out of place. "How are you?"

Wiley released her and patted his chest. "Good as always. Was that Seth Broadhurst in here talking to you?"

"Yes, Dad. I'm catering some hospital functions for him."

"Ahh." Wiley pulled back and studied her, his eyes narrowed. Mimi squirmed, wondering if her condition came with some glaring red sign that advertised her secret. "You look pale. Are you feeling all right?"

"Yes, I just haven't been out in the sun much lately. I've been working a lot. You know how it is."

His eyebrows furrowed together. "You've lost a little weight, too."

Mimi squirmed again. "I guess I haven't been eating as many desserts as I used to. You know, when you bake all day, you don't feel like eating. And I've been practicing for this part on the new soap they're filming in Atlanta."

"Have you seen the van advertising the shop?" Wiley asked. "I passed it on the way here."

"Yes, Dad." Mimi grinned at the pleased look on her father's face. "The big chocolate cake is great."

"Old Jim Bob over in Pickens County owed me a favor." Mimi's mother cleared her throat, and Wiley moved to Mimi's side. "Your mother wanted to come in and say hello."

Mimi took in her appearance, wondering what in the world she was supposed to say to this stranger.

Everything from her mother's sophisticated chignon to her tailored suit spelled money and authority and career woman.

"Hi, Mimi. Since my new office is just down the street, I thought I'd stop by and see you."

How nice of you. Especially as I haven't seen you in years. She bit back the bitter thought and pasted on a smile. "Alison said you're opening a law practice in town. Won't you be bored after living in L.A.?"

Mrs. Hartwell smiled, and for the first time Mimi realized how strongly Hannah resembled their mother. "Actually I'm looking forward to the change of pace. I can't wait to get out of the rat race."

Mimi nodded. *Just like you couldn't wait to escape us.*

"We're going to have some coffee, hon, and talk," her father said.

Mimi turned a questioning look toward her father.

"Business, honey. Your mom's trading in her car."

And she intended to buy one from Wiley? Mimi gaped at her father. She and Hannah and Alison had thought it would be awkward for her mother to return, but it was more than awkward. It was downright weird.

Seth's face flashed into her mind. When their baby grew up, would he or she feel caught in the middle of their strained relationship?

Chapter Eleven

Seth wrestled with his emotions the rest of the week. He approached Thursday, the day he would see Mimi at the support group, with both trepidation and giddiness. He'd hoped she'd had enough space. He'd missed her, her bright smile, her vibrant eyes, her soft voice.

The morning dragged by. By lunchtime he'd already dealt with two seriously ill patients he'd had to commit to the psych ward and his parents, who had nixed every idea he'd put forth during the board meeting. They questioned using grant money to fund the support group. He'd invited them to the session tonight so they could see firsthand the rapport he'd built with his patients and hopefully be convinced of the worthiness of the project.

His last patient of the day had finally shown up. She wanted marriage counseling. Considering his own predicament, he wasn't sure he felt qualified to give it.

"Our marriage fell apart during my first pregnancy." Thirty-five-year-old Doreen Scott leaned back in the leather recliner. "I was sick at first and pretty emotional."

He could relate to that.

"And Bob didn't know what to do. He's a mechanic. He can do anything with a car, but he isn't very good with words."

According to women, most men weren't.

"And I felt like an elephant, so our sex life went downhill. I even worried he might turn to someone else, but I don't think he ever did."

Hadn't Mimi mentioned pregnant women being fat and unattractive? "Did your husband say anything about your looks?" Seth asked. "Or were those your own feelings?"

She tapped her finger on her chin in thought. "Well, no, he never said anything. But I felt awkward, so I didn't encourage him, you know, in the bedroom department."

"It sounds like a communication problem," Seth said. "Sometimes we expect people to understand us when we really need to come out and voice our feelings."

She seemed to mull his comment over. "I guess you're right. After the baby was born, I still felt frumpy and I was tired all the time, nursing the baby and all and, well, we just sort of drifted apart."

"Have you tried to explain your feelings to your husband, Doreen?"

"I tried once or twice, but we'd end up fighting. He accused me of complaining all the time."

Seth sighed. "Perhaps you need to tell him the things you told me. Focus on your own feelings, instead of the things he didn't do to please you. He's probably as confused as you are. Maybe you could plan a special date and make it a romantic evening.''

"You mean I should take the initiative?"

"Sure, why not?"

A smile spread across the woman's face. "You're right. I used to do things to surprise him. I'll try it again."

Mrs. Scott rose and thanked him. Seth said goodbye, hoping her plan worked. As for him, her comments had given him an idea. If Mimi felt insecure about the physical changes pregnancy would bring, he'd show her he understood, that he was sensitive to her needs.

After all, he was responsible for her condition. Maybe they didn't love each other, but they could make things work to smooth the way for the baby.

He sat back, opened a file and began a list of things he could do to convince Mimi to marry him. His methodical approach worked with his job, so why not with his personal life? Finally, after he'd exhausted his brain and come up with several ideas, he turned off his desk lamp, locked his office and headed out to look for the perfect gift to surprise her with. Maybe a book on nursing. And since Mimi liked stylish clothes, he'd find a catalog of the latest maternity fashions.

Yes, that would be perfect. His step felt lighter as he strolled toward the shopping area. Maybe he'd even splurge and buy Mimi a maternity outfit. Not only would she be surprised, she'd love it, and he'd score some personal points with her for being a considerate man.

"THIS IS GOING to make a great bridal shop, Ali. The space is perfect." Mimi thumbed through the catalog of bridal gowns Alison had placed on the counter while her sister pointed out her plans for the near-empty space.

"I'm going to set up a registry in that corner, use that wall for bridal gowns. I'll have three fitting rooms and invitations on that side..."

Mimi laughed as Alison rattled on and on. "Sounds like you've thought of everything."

"I can't wait to open the shop," Alison said. "But it'll take a couple of months to get in all my inventory."

Mimi ran her finger over the photograph of an antique wedding dress dripping with pearls and lace. "I know you'll make a success. Sugar Hill's needed a bridal shop forever."

"I could plan your wedding," Alison offered. "I'd love to have you as my first customer."

Mimi frowned and glanced at her sister's hopeful face. "It's not going to happen, sis. Sorry."

Alison folded her arms and leaned against the workhorse. Paint supplies, color and fabric samples, and work tools filled the half-finished space. "Seth won't marry you?"

"No."

"Creep. And I thought he was high class."

"I meant, no, we're not getting married. He asked. I said no."

"But why?" Alison moved toward her, her brows raised. "He's the father—"

"Shh." Although the room was empty, Mimi glanced around, her palms sweating.

"You have to tell Hannah and Dad, Mimi. You can't keep the truth from them forever."

"I know."

"So Seth did ask you to marry him?"

Mimi closed the bridal book, an image of her wearing the beautiful gown floating through her mind. She'd have lilies, and Hannah and Alison would wear yellow and... She forced the fantasy away. "Yes, he asked, but only because he feels responsible. I don't want a shotgun wedding, Ali."

Alison made a clicking sound with her tongue. "I'm not sure that's what it would be. I saw the way Seth looked at you the other day."

"Oh, yeah. He was probably mortified. I had to run out of the room earlier, and he found me half-dead in the bathroom. I was so nauseated I'm sure I'd turned putrid green."

"He didn't look mortified. He looked protective and infatuated at the same time, like he could gobble you up."

Mimi rolled her eyes. "Trust me, sis. He was not infatuated. He...I think he still has feelings for Hannah."

Alison paused and patted her back. "I never saw him look at Hannah that way."

Mimi shrugged. "She was smart enough not to get pregnant."

"I think he has the hots for you, Mimi. Maybe you should ask him how he feels about Hannah."

Mimi stood and grabbed her purse, a vision of herself in the wedding gown forming in her mind again. Beside her stood Seth, dressed in a black tux, his sandy hair gleaming in the sunlight. But instead of a smile on his face and a ring in his hand, he kicked at the heavy ball and chain attached to his foot.

Mimi fought the image all the way home. After packing supplies for the session, she decided to practice her belly-dance routine before the support group started, so she slipped on her harem costume, stood in front of the mirror and turned on her CD player.

Egyptian music drifted through the air, seeping into her body and transforming her into an erotic princess as she wiggled her hips and jangled her tambourine. When the music finally ended, she studied her reflection, wondering what Seth would think of her slinky outfit. She looked like a genie from a bottle, not a wife or mother. Still, she closed her eyes and momentarily envisioned dancing with him. Watching his gaze fasten on her body as she swayed seductively, hearing his breath catch, feeling his body grow hot.

Suddenly warm herself, she opened her eyes and stared into the mirror. The sexy image faded and she imagined the way she would look in a few months. The harem costume was no longer appealing because her huge belly spilled over the elastic waistband.

The visions changed and blurred, replaced by a mental picture of her wearing the wedding dress she'd admired in the magazine at Alison's shop. She glanced at the hope chest and had a sudden impulse to pretend Seth really loved her, that he really wanted her for his bride. Grateful she was alone, she pulled out the bouquet of flowers Grammy Rose had given her and held them in front of her. Humming the wedding march under her breath, she pretended she and Seth were getting married in the gazebo on her grandmother's mountain just as Hannah and Jake had.

Seth looked at her with love in his eyes, and she felt beautiful, coveted, treasured as his wife. Then they would escape for their wedding night. Seth would have a surprise waiting for her, a slinky black see-though negligee that would bring him to his knees with want. Yes, in her dreams, Seth would choose something sexy, something to prove that he saw her as a woman, not just as his baby's mother.

THE DESSERT SPREAD was fabulous—Mimi had included cookies decorated like animals and cupcakes with sprinkles for the children. But tension radiated between Seth and Mimi. Even the session seemed strained tonight, although Seth couldn't put his finger on the problem.

Maybe the parents and children sensed his parents' presence, their glowering, critical eyes. It was an understatement to say his folks weren't comfortable with the kids who'd attended. In fact, they'd never spent much time with children at all. Including him.

The realization stirred memories of a lonely childhood, of long days without playmates or laughter in his house. He tried to dismiss the unsettling feeling and seated the kids in a circle with their parents.

"Georgie, would you like to tell us how you feel about your parents' divorce?"

Georgie squirmed and spilled fruit punch down his leg. His mother yelped and swiped at the sticky mess with a stack of napkins.

"Anita, why don't you share while Georgie gets cleaned up?" Seth suggested.

The towheaded little girl ducked her head and poked her thumb in her mouth, sucking vigorously.

Parents shifted uncomfortably and whispered to their kids. Two little boys actually tried to hop up and leave. Everyone seemed reluctant to talk tonight.

Seth's own parents spoke to each other in hushed murmurs. They'd never understood why he'd gone into psychiatry instead of surgery or another specialty because they didn't relate to people. Except where their checkbooks were concerned. They'd probably already written off his program as unworthy of funding.

Mimi motioned him to the corner. "Mind if I make a suggestion?"

He certainly had nothing to lose by listening so he said to the group, "Let's take a break, folks. Help yourself to some refreshments, then we'll come back and maybe someone will feel like talking."

The children and parents rushed to get food and drinks, looking relieved. His folks frowned in disapproval.

He jammed his hands in his pockets so he wouldn't touch Mimi. "I don't understand. Last week the parents really opened up."

"You're talking about kids here, Seth. Grown-ups

have trouble sharing their private problems with people in a group, but kids are even more uncomfortable."

He bristled. "And where did you get your child-psychology degree?"

"I don't have one," she said defensively. "But I...I was in a session similar to this once."

"You were?"

"Yes, the counselor at our school organized a divorce group—imagine calling it that and all the other kids knowing. Once a week the principal came on over the intercom and announced for the divorce group to meet in the counselor's office. Everyone would stare at the kids who left the classroom as if they had a big neon sign on their foreheads." She fiddled with a stack of napkins, straightening them.

"Your dad made you go after your mom left?"

She nodded.

He instinctively squeezed her arm, grateful when she didn't pull away. "I'm sorry, Mimi. I didn't realize."

"It was a long time ago."

But not so long ago that the pain didn't still affect her, Seth realized.

"Anyway, it's weird telling strangers how you feel. Kids want to look cool. They think no one else has it the way they do."

Her analysis made sense. "So what do you suggest?"

"How about some fun stories first to break the ice?"

A bead of perspiration trickled down his chin. "I don't know how to tell stories to kids."

"Just let me handle it."

"But what if the kids get out of control?"

Mimi frowned. "Don't worry, they won't. And laughter's good medicine, isn't it?"

"Well, yeah, I suppose."

With a confident smile, she ushered the kids into a circle on the floor. Seth watched in amazement as the group quieted and Mimi sprang into action. She told one story after another, all traditional children's favorites, acting out the characters. She changed the tales slightly, too, making the mama bear and papa bear in "Goldilocks and the Three Bears" live in two separate houses. Before he realized how it had happened, the children and parents all joined in, mimicking the movements and animal sounds. Everyone except his own parents, who were obviously too dignified to participate.

"Dr. Broadhurst, you be the wolf!" Georgie yelled when Mimi began the story of "The Big Bad Wolf."

Seth's mother watched stoically and his father left the room, their disapproval ringing loud and clear. Come to think of it, his parents had never encouraged him to join in the school programs when he was little. They thought music or any recreational activity a waste of time and intelligence. No wonder he'd become so boring as an adult.

"Now," Mimi said after everyone had applauded his performance, "let's do some role playing. Since you're all such good actors and actresses, we'll take turns on stage. Who wants to start?"

The little blond girl raised her hand. "Me, me."

"Great, sweetie." Mimi waved her up to the space she reserved for the playacting and picked out two more kids. "Dr. Broadhurst will tell you a situation, and you guys get to act it out."

The children clapped and Seth realized she'd given him an impromptu warm-up session for role playing. She was brilliant.

The next half hour flew. Each of the children took a turn to participate in a small skit. Seth improvised by making up situations similar to experiences and problems the kids and single parents faced. Parents received an eye-opening experience as they realized firsthand the impact their home lives had on their children. When the evening ended, all the parents thanked him and seemed eager for the next session. His parents left without commenting or even saying goodbye.

Georgie and the other children hugged Mimi. She'd been clearing the tables, but stopped to give each of them a hug. Seth's heart squeezed at the honest affection in her eyes. He could picture her with their baby, holding, cuddling, rocking the child, telling their child stories at bedtime, mesmerizing him or her with her voice and movements, kissing their little one good-night. Unlike the home he'd grown up in, with his nannies and tutors and servants, her house would be filled with love and warmth, with her animals and kindness and her exuberance for life. With love for their baby.

Only, where would he fit into the picture? Would she let him be in the picture at all?

Yes, he thought. He'd make sure he was included.

He thought of the list he'd made on the computer—he'd insist she go for dinner with him tonight, then give her his surprise present. He could hardly wait to see her face when she opened it.

"SETH, THANKS FOR DINNER, but you really didn't have to. This place must be expensive."

"It's worth it."

She bit down on her lip, hoping she wasn't underdressed for the plush surroundings.

"I tried to give you the space you wanted this week."

"I know." Mimi toyed with the rim of her coffee cup, wondering if he'd missed her as much as she'd missed him. She also darted a quick look around the restaurant to make sure her family wasn't there to see them together. "And I appreciate it."

"I wanted to thank you for what you did tonight."

So business had prompted this dinner. She tried not to let her disappointment show. "I simply got the ball rolling. You can handle it fine next time."

"Hey, we make a great team. You are coming next week, aren't you?"

Mimi sipped her decaf coffee. "Yes. Actually I had an idea. I thought you might want to do a session where the children and their parents make the dessert together. What do you think?"

Seth's eyebrows drew together, his frown deepening the way it always did when he lapsed into thought. For some reason Mimi found the habit endearing. Odd how Seth's little nuances had once been unappealing, but now seemed the opposite. "Sounds interesting."

"My grandmother used to cook with me all the time. We'd talk for hours while we tried different recipes."

"Maybe we should try making dinner together some night, and you could show me what you mean."

His sexy smile teased her nerve endings, but Mimi sensed an underlying seriousness in his suggestion. Maybe he was right, maybe they should be friends, especially if they decided to have shared custody. After all, she didn't want their child to feel uncomfortable when they passed him or her back and forth.

The mere idea of what she'd just thought sent a sick feeling to her stomach again.

"Are you okay? You look pale, Mimi."

"No, I'm fine. I…I was just thinking." She averted her gaze, unable to stand the tension between them, the attraction that seemed to grow every time she saw him. She'd tried to avoid thoughts of Seth's dark eyes skating over her all evening, of the way the candlelight flickered during dinner, creating shadows all around his handsome face, the way the soft music in the background reminded her of the night they'd danced together, the night they'd made love.

She wanted him again. Probably hormonal, but what the heck. She couldn't deny those feelings any longer.

He must have sensed her desire, because he ran his thumb over her hand. Gently he lifted it to his mouth, placed his lips on her skin and brought her to a fever pitch of emotions with the tender gesture. His lips traced a path over her palm, then he pressed her hand against his cheek and closed his eyes as if he savored her touch. She licked her lips and saw him open his eyes, heat and fire and hunger shining like a beckoning light. He leaned forward and brushed his lips across her mouth, then nipped at her lip with his teeth until she opened for him. He tasted like spicy marinara sauce and wine and coffee, and smelled of that strong masculine scent she'd tried so hard to forget. He deepened the kiss, the hunger in her belly weakening her resolve to remain uninvolved, and she cupped his jaw with her hand and licked his tongue. The kiss lasted forever, sensual and full of passion, teasing and whispering of hidden hungers and desires they dared not broach.

Finally Seth eased away, his hot breath fanning her cheek as he gently kissed her. "I have something for you," he said softly.

A flutter of excitement stirred to life. "You do?"

He nodded and lay a brightly wrapped gift on the table. The few remaining patrons in the surrounding booths faded into oblivion as Mimi studied the package.

"I wanted you to know that I understand what you're going through, and that I'm here for you, Mimi."

She blinked back tears, moved by his sincerity.

"I hope you understand how I feel when you see what's inside."

Mimi imagined the negligee in her earlier fantasies. A silky nightgown that would caress her body and accentuate every curve, a garment that would entice him to tear it off and love her all over again, the way a man loves a woman he wants forever.

She tore off the paper, her heart thumping in anticipation, then pulled away the tissue paper and saw a thread of black, felt the soft—thick?—material, spattered with sequins.

It wasn't a negligee at all. Her hand froze as she spotted the label, and disappointment slammed into her. He hadn't bought her a sexy present at all. He'd bought her what had to be the biggest, ugliest maternity blouse in the world. And underneath the hideous thing he'd included a book. *Tips for the Nursing Mother.*

Chapter Twelve

Seth watched in horror as Mimi ran from the table. Her face had paled as soon as she'd opened the gift. Was she sick again? He drummed his fingers on the table and told himself to wait, but as the seconds ticked by, his anxiety grew. He couldn't simply sit here if she needed something.

Decision made, he tossed his napkin on the table and crossed the room, halting at the door to the ladies' room. Would he be forever chasing her into ladies' rooms?

He knocked gently and called her name, but a thin blond woman exited.

"Did you happen to see a woman go in there?" he asked.

"There are several women in there. It is a ladies' room."

His voice sounded shaky, but he forged ahead. "She has long, auburn hair and she's wearing a short, dark-blue dress."

The woman looked down her patrician nose at him. "What did you do to her?"

"What?"

"She's in there sobbing her heart out."

"What?"

"You heard me." She pushed past him. "Poor girl's going to make herself sick."

His adrenaline kicked in and he stormed through the door, scanning the room for Mimi. A heavy brunette adjusting her panty hose shrieked, and an elderly woman batted him with her alligator purse. "Help! Call security!"

"Wait! I'm harmless." He threw up his hands, partly in surrender, partly to protect himself. "I'm looking for my...my girlfriend."

The brunette lunged from the bathroom. The elderly woman squinted at him over her wire rims. "You're not here to rob us?"

"No, I'm a doctor! I came to check on my girlfriend."

"What'd you do to her?"

Why did everyone assume he'd hurt her? "I think she's ill."

"Seth?"

He gazed past the woman, who turned an evil look his way as she hobbled out, and saw Mimi staring at him, her eyes red and swollen.

Alarm clanged in his head. "What's wrong?"

"What are you doing in here?" Mimi asked at the same time.

"I came to see if you were okay." He ran a hand through his hair in frustration. "Are you sick again?"

She shook her head and brushed past him to the vanity area, taking her compact from her purse and beginning to powder her nose. "I think you should leave."

"Not until you tell me what the hell's going on. I was worried about you. I expected to come in and find you passed out, then these women practically accosted me and—"

"You think I'm going to be a big fat blob."

"What?"

"You said that gift showed what you thought of me, and you bought me a hideous humongous tent to wear. And a book on nursing."

"Hideous? I thought you'd like it. You wear black skirts all the time, and it has those shiny sequin things, and I told you I hate skinny women, and I wasn't sure if you'd decided about nursing—"

"I haven't. And that blouse looks like a clown suit."

"It came from the most expensive maternity shop in Atlanta. I hunted all day to find something I thought you'd like."

"Well, that shows how much you know about me."

"At least I tried."

"What's that supposed to mean?"

Seth ran a hand over his neck, frustrated. "Look, I know we're in an awkward situation, but I'm trying to be mature and responsible—"

"And you're saying I'm not?"

"No. I thought you were worried about gaining weight, and I got you in this condition and you like clothes, so I thought a new top might cheer you up." Good grief, he was starting to babble just like Mimi.

Mimi finger-combed her hair and said, her voice husky, "Don't you get it, Seth? I don't want you hovering over me because you feel responsible or feel sorry for me."

He sighed at the slight tremble in her voice. "I apologize. I really thought you'd like the gift."

Mimi gulped. "Then next time get me something sexy, not something four people could fit into."

"You wanted something sexy?" He would never understand female logic. Sex had gotten them into this situation in the first place.

"No. Yes." She turned and took her lipstick from her purse. A young woman walked in with her toddler daughter and halted, her eyes wide. She grabbed her daughter's hand and started to leave, but Seth held up his hand.

"No, don't leave," he said, lowering his voice. "I'm going. I'll wait outside for you, Mimi." He shoved his hands in his pockets and stalked from the room, not bothering to wait for her reply.

MIMI FELT A SURGE of guilt as Seth drove her home. He hadn't spoken a word since they'd left the restaurant. The tension grated on her frayed nerves. Somewhere between the bathroom and the car she realized she'd overreacted in a major way. Although misguided in his tastes, Seth had been sincere with his gift. He really needed to work on his taste in clothing, though. And learn hers. Maybe she should try to get along with him. After all, they were having a baby together.

God, the baby would change her life in so many

ways. Her body, her daily routine, her career... She was simply having trouble dealing with it all at once. And dealing with Seth.

They were far too different to ever have a relationship. They knew nothing about each other. They weren't only Mars-Venus, they were from different galaxies.

Then why did she find him so incredibly attractive lately? Almost boyishly appealing, and the way his eyes drooped with disappointment reminded her a little of a cocker spaniel. She was a sucker for those dogs.

She struggled for words, wanting to apologize, as he pulled into the drive. "Seth, I...I'm sorry."

He killed the engine and turned toward her, his expression unreadable. But a flicker of emotion caught in his eyes, trapping her.

"I admit I overreacted, and I know you were trying to be nice, and I shouldn't have gotten so upset about the maternity blouse—"

"You can take the damn thing back. I know you hate it."

She reached for his hand and curled her fingers around his, a warm sensation skittering up her spine when the corner of his mouth lifted into the barest hint of a smile.

"It wasn't that I hated it—"

He arched a brow.

"Okay, well, I did hate it. Did you like it?"

He shrugged "Not really, but I thought you liked wild stuff."

"Not tentlike wild stuff."

He muttered something about females. He really didn't have a clue. She'd just have to spell it out.

"What really upset me, Seth, was that that's how you saw me." Her voice grew soft. "As a pregnant woman, not…"

His dark gaze raked her. "How do you want me to see you, Mimi?"

She shrugged, feeling uncharacteristically shy. And very vulnerable. "Not as a big blob of fat."

He chuckled. "As the mother of my baby?"

"Not just that, either."

She closed her eyes, knowing she'd revealed more than she should, but letting the silence stretch between them. His thumb brushed her chin and she opened her eyes. "I see you, Mimi. And I think you're beautiful."

The breath collected in her lungs as his deep husky voice skated over her.

"And sexy and vibrant." He angled his head and leaned toward her, his breath whispering against her cheek. "And kind and funny." He tucked a strand of hair behind her ear. "And amazingly unpredictable and provocative…" His voice trailed off as his tongue found better things to do, like tracing a line down her jaw, sweeping along her lips, pushing into her mouth with a hunger that dove straight to her middle.

Mimi arched against him, clinging to him, matching the kiss with a yearning all her own. His fingers combed through the thick strands of her hair, and he dragged her closer. She leaned into the hard wall of his chest and moaned. He cupped her face and bestowed kisses on her cheeks, her forehead, her chin, then dipped his head to explore the sensitive skin behind her ear, her neck, then lower. Mimi's body ached, tightened with need. She strained for his touch, the warmth in her abdomen spreading through her like a flash flood of desire.

Suddenly a car horn blasted behind them and they leaped apart. Mimi glanced over her shoulder and Seth groaned.

"Your family again?" he asked. "Is every Thursday night check-in time?"

"I don't know, but I can't let them see us like this. What would they think?" Mimi straightened her clothing and hair in a panic.

Seth stared at her, his expression hooded again. "They have to find out sometime, Mimi."

Mimi's heartbeat accelerated. Before she could reply, she heard someone tapping on the window. Seth pushed the automatic-release button and the window slid down.

"Hey." Alison poked her head in as Hannah and Wiley strolled up the drive toward the car. "What are you two up to?" Mimi didn't miss the mischievous grin on her younger sister's face.

"Talking. What are you doing here?" Mimi asked. "You didn't tell Dad, did you?"

Alison shook her head, her eyes twinkling. "Jake had to go to work and Hannah was lonely, so she stopped by Dad's. Dad suggested we come to see you. If I'd known you were 'parking,' I'd—"

Mimi glared at her sister, silencing her, then saw the worried expression on Hannah's face as she approached. Surely Hannah hadn't told their father about her pregnancy.

Hannah appeared at the window and Mimi opened the door and climbed out. Seth exited the driver's side and spoke to her father, following him to the porch swing.

"What are you doing with Seth?" Hannah asked.

Mimi almost panicked. Did Hannah know the truth? "He drove me home from that support-group session I'm catering on Thursday nights."

Hannah nodded, her gaze settling past Mimi to the inside of the car. Mimi saw the book Hannah was staring at, *Tips for the Nursing Mother,* and winced.

"You told Seth?" Hannah asked.

Mimi's stomach quivered with nerves. Seth strode back toward the car at the same time, his expression odd as he watched her.

"Yes, he knows."

Hannah smiled. "I'm glad you decided to talk to someone, Mimi. Seth's a great listener."

Seth quirked an eyebrow at Mimi, and she felt like crawling under the floormats. Of course Hannah would know he was a great listener, because she'd been with him first. How could Seth not compare her with Hannah?

"Thanks for being there for my sister, Seth," Hannah said softly. "I appreciate your friendship."

Seth simply nodded, his eyes dark. Mimi faked a smile, hurt and confusion once again suffusing her. Seth was only taking care of her because she was pregnant. How could she have been so stupid to have fallen for his kiss?

"Yeah, Seth, thanks for the counseling and for the ride." With a quick wave, Mimi hurried up the sidewalk, faintly aware that Alison had given her a murderous look as if she was a coward, and that Seth's dark gaze had been filled with something that almost looked like disappointment. But that couldn't be, she thought as she ran up the porch to meet her father. Seth didn't want Hannah to know he'd fathered her baby, either, or he would have spoken up. Wouldn't he?

SETH FOUGHT DISAPPOINTMENT as he drove away from Mimi's. Mimi had had the perfect opportunity to tell Hannah and her family about the two of them, to correct Hannah's false assumption about their baby's paternity. But she'd lied and treated him like an outsider. As her *counselor,* for God's sake.

As if he didn't have a personal, somewhat emotional investment in their future or their child. As if he would never be a part of her close-knit family.

Something he'd never wanted before now, he realized as he drove in circles around the city, avoiding going back to his lonely, quiet house. To the cold steel-gray carpet and colorless rooms. To his empty bed. Alone.

Of course, he could visit his own family. Spend some quality time with them.

A sardonic chuckled escaped him. Who was he kidding? His family wasn't close, never had been. He'd feel as comfortable in a bar filled with strangers as he would with his own parents, and he'd be a hell of a lot more likely to spill his troubles to an anonymous bartender than to his emotionless folks. He yanked at his tie, remembering the warm, loving way Mimi had opened her arms to the children and invited them into her heart without a moment's hesitation.

Why couldn't Mimi open her arms and learn to care about him the same way?

MIMI'S LEGS wobbled as she faced her father. She didn't know how he knew about the pregnancy, but she realized he did.

He gripped her hand in his chubby one. "Honey, I had to come and see you."

Hannah settled into the armchair in the den, while Alison sprawled in the beanbag chair. Mimi gave Hannah a questioning look. Hannah shook her head as if to deny telling their father about her pregnancy.

"Don't worry, your sisters haven't spilled your secrets. Not that I didn't ask." Wiley scratched his neck, looking oddly uncomfortable. "I saw how pale you've been lately, though, and put two and two together."

"But how did you know?"

"I've been there three times, sugar. I'd recognize the signs anywhere."

Mimi sank onto the sofa, wondering now why she'd chosen leather. It was cold and she was shaking. "Dad—"

Wiley held up a hand. "Let me say something first."

Mimi bit down on her lip.

"I love you, sweetheart, no matter what. And I don't care what happened, who...well, I don't have to know the details. But you'll always be my baby and I'll always be here for you."

Mimi's eyes filmed with tears. "Daddy, I...I'm sorry. I wanted to tell you but..." Her voice broke and she brushed at the tears in her eyes. "I didn't want you to be disappointed in me."

"How could I be when I'm so proud of you?" He enveloped her in a hug, and within seconds Hannah and Alison joined in, all crying and laughing at the same time.

Finally they pulled apart and Wiley grinned. "When is my grandbaby going to be here?"

Mimi laughed in spite of her tears. "In the fall."

"Autumn. My favorite time of year." Wiley's smile faded slightly, and he shifted onto his heels, staring at his white loafers. "Are you all right, hon? Everything check out okay?"

"I examined her myself, Dad," Hannah said softly. "Everything's fine."

"Other than the fact that I'm not married," Mimi whispered.

Wiley frowned. "You want me to see about getting Joey out of jail?"

Mimi gaped at him. After everything Joey had done to hurt him, her father would actually help him get an early release if she asked. She saw Alison's knowing look and the fear that flickered briefly in Hannah's eyes. She couldn't go on allowing her family to believe Joey had fathered her baby, not after the way he'd hurt their family.

Seth's face flashed into her mind—had he wanted

her to tell them the truth? *They have to find out some-time,* he'd said. He was right. It might as well be now.

She gestured toward the sofa and chairs. "Listen, you guys. I think you'd better sit down. I have something important to tell you."

Chapter Thirteen

Seth had just settled down to a lonely overdone TV dinner when the doorbell rang. He imagined Mimi showing up at his door, prepared to pick up where they'd left off, and his heart skipped a beat.

It stopped completely when he looked through the peephole and saw Mimi's father standing there. Disappointment ballooned in his chest, a case of nerves rapidly following.

He had never seen such an earnest look on the burly, outrageous man's face before. If he didn't know better, he'd think Wiley knew about his situation with Mimi. But he did know better. Mimi had lied through her teeth to her family. She'd thanked him for counseling, then dismissed him as if he was little more than a stranger. If she'd told her dad about her pregnancy, she'd probably let him believe Joey had fathered the baby.

Maybe that was the reason Wiley had come, for counseling—or to discuss Joey.

The doorbell rang again and he stopped his silent diatribe and opened the door.

Wiley didn't waste time on pleasantries. He strode

in, his lime-green jacket flapping about him, his white shoes clicking on the hardwood foyer. "Can we talk?"

"Sure." Seth motioned toward the study where he did most of his work and serious thinking, psycho-analyzing, as Mimi would call it. Wiley certainly looked serious. "Can I get you a drink? Coffee?"

"Whiskey would be good."

Seth nodded and poured him a generous shot, then watched as Wiley downed the amber liquid and paced across the oak-paneled room. Seth had just picked up the decanter to offer him another when Wiley spoke. "I hear you and my daughter are going to have a baby together."

The decanter nearly slipped from Seth's hand. He regained his grip just in time.

"She told you?" For a reason he didn't understand, he felt like grinning. He must have done so, because Wiley arched his bushy brows.

"You're happy about it?"

"I'm glad she finally told you."

"What about the baby?"

Seth shrugged. "It was a shock at first. But the idea's growing on me."

Wiley took the decanter and poured himself another shot, then poured one for Seth and pointed to the wing chairs flanking the brick fireplace. Seth followed Wiley's silent command and sat down.

"Wanna tell me what you're going to do?"

"I…I'll do whatever's necessary to take care of the situation."

Wiley frowned and stood, his eyes gleaming with

fury. "What do you mean, whatever's necessary? You're not trying to talk my daughter into not having the baby, are you?"

"No," Seth said, shocked. "I didn't mean that at all."

"'Cause that's flat out of the question. Mimi loves kids and animals and wouldn't hurt a fly."

"I agree."

"That baby's gonna need a daddy."

"I agree with that, too."

"You do?"

"Absolutely. I...I think we should get married."

Wiley's face registered surprise. "Mimi didn't mention you'd talked marriage."

"What did she tell you—that she thought I'd run out on my responsibility?"

"No, uh, I kind of left before we really discussed it."

He'd come over looking for a confrontation. Seth took a long pull of his own drink, frustration drawing his fingers tightly around his glass. "That's because she hasn't agreed to marry me yet."

"What do you mean? You have asked her, haven't you?"

"Yes. But she refuses. She even let Hannah think the baby was that hoodlum Joey's."

Wiley made a clicking sound with his tongue. "Well, she cleared that up a few minutes ago."

A sigh of relief escaped Seth. "Did she say anything about her feelings for me?"

Wiley shook his head. "Nope. But you have to convince her to get married. I don't want my grandbaby to be brought into this world without his father's name. I know that sounds old-fashioned, but I reckon I am old-fashioned when it comes to my little girls.''

Seth understood. If his own irrational behavior of late was any indication of how he'd be as a father, he had a feeling he'd be as protective and old-fashioned with his daughters as Wiley was of his. He finished his drink and stood, gazing into the vacant fireplace, imagining a fire glowing in the hearth, Mimi's warm laughter filling the emptiness. Their little girl cuddled by the fire holding a book, their son waiting with a baseball for Seth to play catch with him. Or maybe his daughter had the baseball...

''I've been trying to get close to her,'' he said, his voice thick, ''but she keeps pushing me away. The first time we talked, she said she was against marriage completely.''

''Really? That's odd.''

''Actually it's not.'' Mimi's comments about her parents' marriage sifted through his foggy brain. He thought about the kids of divorced parents he counseled, the way Mimi had instinctively understood the children's needs. ''You see, Mr. Hartwell, I think Mimi saw what happened with your marriage and it scared her.''

Wiley looked stricken.

Seth hesitated, hating to talk about Wiley's personal life. He also felt as if he was breaching a patient's confidentiality, although Mimi wasn't a patient. Still, her parents' situation was important. ''She told me you only married Mrs. Hartwell because she was pregnant with Hannah.''

Wiley's stunned face turned to him.

"Since you two ended up hating each other, she's convinced we'd be the same way."

"Damn." Wiley dropped his face into his hands. "I had no idea the girls knew."

Seth lay a hand on Wiley's shoulder. "I'm sorry. But Mimi told me that she and Hannah heard you two arguing the day Mrs. Hartwell left. It must have been traumatic for them."

Wiley nodded, looking miserable. "My poor little girls. I can't believe they never said anything."

"They love you, Wiley."

Wiley's face was almost ashen as he studied Seth. "Tell me, son, what are we going to do about all this?"

Seth leaned against the bookshelf. "I'm going to convince Mimi that we can make it, that she has to give us a chance."

"What have you done so far?"

Seth described his plan, how he'd enlisted Mimi's help with the support group and how successful their working arrangement had been, then confessed about the gift. "I thought I was buying something she'd like, but she hated it."

Wiley chuckled. "Let me clue you in, son. Three rules to please a woman. Number one—she's always right. Number two—if she asks you if she looks fat, you say no. You don't stop to think about it, you just blurt it out. And number three—go for more personal gifts, something she can use to pamper herself."

"Like a gift certificate to a gym?"

Wiley shook his head. "You have a long way to

go, boy. Think romantic stuff like perfume, all that smelly bath stuff women like, a day at a spa."

"Oh, I see what you're saying."

"And jewelry."

"Something like those clunky earrings she wears?"

"No, diamonds. Although there's something even more important to Mimi."

"What's that?"

"Her animals. You have to love all those little scrappy, homely things she brings home."

Seth reached for the scotch. He was in trouble. *Things* he could buy. But animals… Her dog, Wrangler, hated him, and he'd never been comfortable with any kind of four-legged creature.

"I'm sorry, Hannah." Mimi twisted her fingers together and paced across the den. "I know this is awkward and I don't want you to hate me."

Hannah jerked as if coming out of shock. "I…I don't hate you. Why would I hate you?"

When Alison nodded encouragement, Mimi took a deep breath and continued, "Because you were engaged to Seth and we've never dated each other's boyfriends before, past or present, and it was only one night, and now I've made such a freaking mess of things!"

Hannah gripped Mimi's arms to calm her. "Mimi, it's all right. Seth's a wonderful guy and, well, other than the fact that you two got it backward and got pregnant before you married, well, I couldn't be happier for you or him."

"But we're not getting married."

"You're not?" Hannah tapped her foot, then glanced at Alison for confirmation.

Alison shrugged. "She thinks he's still in love with you."

"What?"

"Alison!" Mimi glared at her younger sister.

"Well, you do."

Mimi pressed her hands over her cheeks. "You weren't supposed to tell Hannah."

Hannah frowned. "Mimi, did Seth tell you that?"

Mimi hesitated. Oh, hell, might as well get everything out in the open. "Well, no, not exactly. But he didn't want you to know we'd been together."

"He probably thought it would be awkward," Alison offered.

"He said we were a mistake," Mimi continued.

"That doesn't mean he's in love with *me*." Hannah took Mimi's hands and coaxed her to the sofa. "Listen to me, sis. Seth and I had a long talk at the hospital before I married Jake. Seth admitted that he realized we were just friends, that we weren't meant to be together."

"Really?"

"Really. The passion wasn't there, not the way it is with Jake."

"Seth looks at you that way, Mimi." Alison rolled her eyes. "Actually it's pretty disgusting to watch, but I think he really has the hots for you."

Hannah's eyebrows shot up. "That's great, Mimi. I think you and Seth would be wonderful together. I know you'd be good for him."

"But we're complete opposites."

"Sometimes opposites attract," Alison said.

"Seth needs someone to bring out the fun side of him," Hannah added. "To make him laugh."

"But what if he's always comparing me with you?" Mimi said, finally voicing her biggest fear. "You know, in bed?"

"Seth and I never slept together," Hannah said. Mimi's eyes widened, and Hannah continued. "The chemistry just wasn't there. I think we both knew it. That's one of the reasons I called off the wedding."

"Really?"

"Really. So if you have feelings for him, don't be afraid to take a chance. Go for it."

Did she have feelings for Seth? Mimi gripped her sister's hands. Although the reason Seth might be pursuing her still plagued her, a spark of hope suddenly ignited within her. "Still, I couldn't marry Seth, not just because of the baby."

The silent truth hung between Mimi and Hannah—they had overheard their parents' horrible argument the day their mother had deserted them. Hannah opened her mouth to protest, but bit down on her lip, apparently conceding Mimi's point. Even Hannah couldn't deny the reality of how their forced marriage had ended. If Mimi married Seth for the wrong reasons, she would only be repeating the cycle.

"Maybe he's really in love with you," Alison said.

"Yeah, you are awfully lovable," Hannah added with a grin.

Mimi glanced first at Alison, then at Hannah, almost afraid to hope. But Hannah was right; she shouldn't let fear hold her back. Maybe the next time she and Seth were together, she'd look for some sign that he really cared, that he wasn't simply trying to be responsible.

As soon as Wiley left, Seth pulled out his laptop and typed up his plan to win Mimi. They'd have to sign up for childbirth classes—would Mimi want natural childbirth?—and fix a room for the baby. He had two extra bedrooms; maybe he'd go shopping and buy baby furniture and surprise her. And names—they'd have to think of names. Did Mimi hope for a girl or boy?

His talk with Wiley flitted through his mind, and he realized he was once again jumping the gun. What had Wiley said? Romance. He'd never been good at that. Surely there were books out there to help him with romance, too. He was nothing if not a researcher. Quickly accessing the Internet, he pulled up listings on an on-line bookstore and browsed the titles. To his amazement, he found a wide selection ranging from tips for romantic dates to tips for incredible sex. Wow. He'd never noticed them before. He scanned the contents and ordered two of the tamer sounding books, then decided what the hell—if Mimi thought he was boring, he'd order one of the sex-tip ones, and maybe he'd pick up some pointers. After completing the order, he returned to his list.

Romance. Flowers came to mind. He'd order roses for her tomorrow. Maybe they were clichéd and un-original, but they always worked in the movies. And perfume—he'd ask Hannah the name of that exotic fragrance Mimi wore, the one that had made him dizzy the first time they'd been together, then he'd pick up a bottle. And he'd get her some bubble bath, too.

He pictured Mimi lying in a sea of bubbles, her naked skin glistening with water droplets, her wild hair spiraling around her damp face, her cheeks glowing pink from the heat of the bath, him climbing into the water beside her, dipping his hand to stroke her secret places, tasting the salt of her skin, ducking beneath the bubbles to—

He jerked upright, the images so vivid his body reacted in accord. He wanted her with an ache that hammered through his very being. Wanted her the way he'd never wanted any woman before.

He wouldn't wait until tomorrow. He'd do some on-line shopping and have the flowers to her by breakfast. He'd get new underwear for himself, too, some of that skimpy stuff she'd think was exciting, instead of his normal white briefs. Maybe a few pairs of colorful men's bikini briefs or some silk boxers— he supposed he could suffer wearing them if it impressed Mimi.

But he'd search for an on-line store that sold them, so he wouldn't have to embarrass himself by actually going into a store to buy them. After all, a man did have his limits—even for romance.

Chapter Fourteen

"Thank you for the flowers." Mimi covered the phone to hide her sneeze, hoping to avoid telling Seth about her allergic reaction to roses. After all, he'd been so thoughtful to send them to her at the café.

"I'm glad you received them. I hope the florist did a good job."

"They're beautiful." Another sneeze. "Yellow's my favorite color."

"That's good to know," Seth said, his voice teasing. "I'll make a note of it."

Mimi laughed and waved at a familiar customer, grateful the morning rush hour had passed so she could take a break.

"I'm glad you told your family about us."

Mimi perched a hip on a stool, looking for the signs she hoped to find, signs that he cared about her.

"And that I'm the father of the baby."

She tried not to feel disappointed at his statement. "They took it better than I thought."

"Even Hannah?"

The bell jingled behind her, announcing another customer, but she didn't bother to look up. The other waitress could handle the customer. "Yes, even Hannah. You were really worried about her reaction, weren't you?"

He hesitated. "I didn't want her to think I'd used you, Mimi. That I'd been careless with her little sister. She's pretty protective of you, you know."

Mimi smiled, some of her fear dissipating. He sounded sincere. "Yeah, she is. She's been as much a parent to me as a sister."

Someone cleared her throat behind her, and Mimi glanced over her shoulder to see her mother. A small, tight smile flitted across Mrs. Hartwell's face. Mimi closed her eyes and mentally groaned. What was her mom doing here?

"Can I see you later?" Seth asked.

"I...I don't know. I have to go."

"Why, is something wrong?"

"No, just a customer."

"Have you been busy this morning?"

"Swamped. My feet are killing me."

"Are you sure you feel up to working? If you want to take time off and rest, if you, um, need the money, I'll take care of things."

Mimi gaped at the phone. Had she heard Seth correctly? He was offering to let her leave work, maybe quit, and he'd pay for her, like some...some..

"You don't need to be on your feet all day, so you could just resign," he continued. "I make a good salary here at the hospital."

Anger sliced through Mimi again. If she'd been looking for signs, he'd just handed them to her. He saw her and the baby as a package deal, a debt he needed to take care of. Well, she might need his help later, logically of course, but she was self-sufficient right now. She stifled a sneeze and shoved the roses to the end of the counter. "No, thank you, Dr. Broadhurst. I like my job and I have no intention of becoming a kept woman." With a sigh of disgust, she slammed down the phone, blinking back tears as she turned to see what her mother wanted.

SETH LET THE PHONE slide from his ear, his mind reeling. What the hell had just happened?

One minute she'd been all sweet and nice, thanking him for the flowers, and they'd actually been talking about things, actually making headway in their rocky relationship, then the next she'd snapped his head off. He'd simply been trying to be considerate again, thinking of her condition, wanting to take care of her. Why would wanting to relieve her of one area of stress make her angry?

A knock jerked him from his troubled thoughts and he called, "Come in."

Eleanor Bainbridge stepped through the door. "Hi. I've been trying to catch up with you. I wanted to see if we could get together."

Seth noticed her smile and realized she was interested in him. Flattery spiked his pride. But even though Eleanor was attractive, he felt absolutely no spark of attraction to her. "I've been pretty busy," he said, trying to maintain a professional tone. "Is there something specific you needed?"

"No, I wondered if you had time to show me some fun spots in town."

"I'm sorry, but I'm pretty booked now." He hesitated, wondering if he should mention he had a girlfriend. Except technically Mimi wasn't his girlfriend. She was…the mother of his child, his future wife. No, it seemed premature to introduce her that way.

An enigma would be the most apt description. Or the woman who was driving him crazy.

"All right, then. If you do free up some time, give me a call."

Another tap and Hannah Hartwell—no, Hannah *Tippins* appeared in the doorway. Eleanor dropped a card on his desk with her phone number scrawled on top. He opened his mouth to explain to Hannah but had no idea what to say.

"Can we talk for a minute?" Hannah asked.

Dr. Bainbridge flitted her hand in a wave. "I'll see you later, Seth. Don't forget to call when you have time."

Seth nodded and pushed the papers around on his desk, aware of Hannah's astute gaze. "Come on in, Hannah. I've been expecting you."

Eleanor closed the door behind her and Hannah folded her arms across her chest. "What's up with her?"

"Nothing."

She raised a brow. "Really?"

"I'm not interested in Dr. Bainbridge, Hannah. Lord knows, I've got my hands full with…with your sister."

Hannah smiled that understanding smile, and he realized now the reason they'd been friends. They understood each other—which was the opposite of the relationship he had with her sister.

"Mimi told me about you two," Hannah began.

"I don't want you to think I used her."

She held up a hand. "You don't have to explain, Seth."

"But I want you to believe me. It just happened. One minute we were talking and she was telling me about Joey, and we were in the car all alone..." He jumped up and paced in front of his window, running a hand over his neck. "And I kept smelling that damn perfume of hers—it makes me crazy—and then we got stranded and we ate dessert, and she's just so damn sexy, the way she eats chocolate, and then we danced and... God." He dropped his head into his hands. "I'm babbling. I can't believe it, I'm actually babbling."

Hannah laughed. Not a soft little giggle, either. She threw back her head and laughed hysterically.

He raised his head and frowned at her. "What the hell's so funny?"

She covered her mouth in an attempt to control herself, but more laughter sputtered. "I..."

He continued to frown at her. "I'm glad my misery's so entertaining."

She finally gained some semblance of control, but her eyes danced with mischief. "You're in love with her, aren't you."

"Huh?"

She pointed a finger at him. "You, Dr. Seth Broadhurst, the unflappable, methodical, scientific, list-making, genius psychiatrist, are in love with my little sister.''

He gulped. In love with Mimi?

Sure, he *liked* her and she was sexy and probably the kindest, warmest-hearted *real* person he'd ever known, and he grew hot and all mushy just thinking about her.

Dear Lord. Could she be right? No, Seth Broadhurst was too levelheaded to fall in love, not the Hollywood kind of love, anyway. He ran a hand through his hair. ''I do care about Mimi, Hannah. I'm not sure I'd call it love, but I want to try to make a relationship work for the baby.''

Hannah tapped her chin with her finger. ''And that message came through loud and clear to Mimi?''

He winced.

Hannah walked over and gave him a hug, pulling back to study his face. ''Deny it all you want, Seth, but I do think you love my sister. You just don't realize it yet. And I couldn't be happier for you. Mimi's wonderful, but she's always selling herself short. I knew one day someone special would come along and see how fantastic she really is.''

Seth simply stared at her. He'd never been in love before...and no, he wasn't now. Hannah must still be so caught up in her new husband she was romanticizing the situation.

But he had been acting foolishly lately—buying wild underwear, reading books about romance. Babbling nonsense. Now she had him psychoanalyzing himself. He had to focus on the issue at hand—the baby.

"Personal feelings aside, there's still a major problem," he said.

"I know. The pregnancy."

"No." He shook his had emphatically. "I won't let anyone call our baby a problem."

"Good." Hannah grinned. "Then what's the problem?"

"Mimi doesn't want me."

"I wouldn't bet on that," Hannah said with a mischievous glint in her eyes. "I have a feeling she may be madly in love with you, too. She just doesn't know it yet, either."

"No, you don't understand. Everything I do is wrong. Just this morning I sent her a dozen yellow roses—"

"You sent her roses?"

"Yeah." Seth shrugged, slightly embarrassed. "I know it's clichéd, but it always works on TV."

"Flowers are sweet," she admitted with a grin. "But unfortunately Mimi's allergic to roses. I'd better order some topical cream for her. She can't take her normal allergy pills with the pregnancy."

"Good grief, I sent her something that could hurt her."

"Relax, she has a simple sneezing reaction and a few hives. It's no big deal."

Seth slapped his leg in frustration. "Why didn't she tell me she was allergic? I would have sent the damn things back and ordered something else. I'm calling the florist right away. I'll send her mums or—"

"She's allergic to those, too."

"Well, what isn't she allergic to?"

"Lilies. She loves lilies."

"Okay, I'll send her a hundred lilies. Hell, I'll start her a whole garden." He reached for the phone, but Hannah stopped him.

She was laughing again. "You want to know why she didn't tell you about her allergy?"

"Because she thinks I'm an imbecile?"

"No, because she was impressed and she's too much of a softy to hurt your feelings." His chest automatically swelled. *Finally* he'd done something right.

He chuckled sardonically. "Well, she certainly wasn't worried about my feelings when she hung up on me."

"Why did she hang up?"

"She was talking about how busy the place was and how her feet were hurting, and I suggested she take time off work, that I'd pay for her to stay home so she could rest."

"You did what?"

"I offered to support her. I am the father of this baby and I don't think she should be waitressing during the next few months."

Hannah winced. "Uh-oh."

"I know I goofed. I just don't know exactly what I did wrong. I was only trying to take care of her, but she got so emotional." The very reason he and Hannah had been such good friends was that Hannah was calm and rational. But there had never been that passion with her; with Mimi the passion was everything.

Hannah patted him on the back. "Seth, sit down and let me explain something about Mimi..."

Seth listened to his second lesson on women from another Hartwell. Really, he thought, when Hannah had finished explaining Mimi's logic, they should teach a class on understanding women. Maybe he'd look for a book on the Internet tonight, a basic one for the emotionally and romantically impaired, something like *Understanding Women for Dummies*.

"So, MOTHER, what brings you here?"

Mrs. Hartwell studied Mimi, her eyes steady. Her mother had obviously overheard her comment about Hannah being like a mother, but Mimi wouldn't—no, she *couldn't*—apologize for speaking the truth.

"I think we should talk," Mrs. Hartwell said.

Surely her mother didn't know... "I'm working now."

Mrs. Hartwell glanced around the nearly empty café. "It looks as if the other waitress has things under control."

"I'm the manager, Mom, not just a waitress."

"Oh, I'm sorry. I didn't realize."

"You wouldn't. Maybe we can get together some other time?"

"I'd like to talk to you now." Her mother reached out to touch her, but Mimi stepped away. An instinctive reaction. She hadn't seen her mother in years, and now she wanted to chat like friends?

"I can't imagine what's so important."

"*You* are what's important." Her mother's voice sounded firm. Almost *motherly*.

Mimi's breath caught. But her mother didn't have an ounce of mothering instinct in her. "Why now when I'm at work? Why not when it's more convenient?''

"I thought this place might be more neutral. I wasn't sure you'd welcome me into your apartment." Her voice quivered slightly. "You really are important to me, honey."

Mimi felt herself wavering. She was too damn softhearted; she'd get hurt again. "I never was before. None of us were."

Mrs. Hartwell sighed shakily. "Okay, I deserved that. But I still want you to hear me out."

Mimi hesitated, then finally conceded. She might as well get it over with, although she did not need to deal with this today, not on top of everything else. Besides, she had enough interfering family members; she'd been expecting to see her dad in here all morning. He and her sisters would probably set up shifts to watch her the next few months.

"Mimi?"

"Let's take a booth. Can I get you some coffee?"

Her mother ordered a cappuccino, and Mimi chose a fruit juice from the refrigerator and joined her in the far corner, taking her time to study her mother as she sat down. She looked serious, worried even. Less standoffish. Maybe because she was wearing simple black slacks and a purple sweater, instead of one of her expensive tailored suits.

"Your father stopped by to see me last night."

Mimi tore off the cap to her drink, her hands trembling. She did not have a good feeling about the direction of the conversation.

"He told me about…about the baby."

"What?" The bottle of juice clunked onto the laminated tabletop. "He had no right."

"He had every right. I'm your mother."

Mimi simply stared at her. "My mother left me years ago."

Mrs. Hartwell's expression wilted. "I know I deserve that and I'm not here to ask forgiveness—"

"Good."

"But I do care about you."

"Listen, Janelle," Mimi said, purposely using her mother's first name, "if you cared so much, why did you stay away so long?"

Mrs. Hartwell stirred sweetener into her cappuccino, hurt flickering in her eyes. "I wanted to come back a few times, but...well, I was so busy building my career and then I'd waited so long and then...well, I figured it was too late. That you girls hated me, and frankly I was too ashamed of what I'd done."

Mimi's throat felt thick. "Then why are you here now?"

Mrs. Hartwell's gaze rose to meet hers, and Mimi flinched at the torment she saw in her eyes. "Because I'm probably the only one who knows how you're feeling right now. How confused you must be."

Mimi studied her fingernails. She couldn't argue with that.

"Wiley told me that you girls overheard our argument the day I left, that you found out that we had married because I was pregnant with Hannah."

"How did Dad know? We never told him."

Mrs. Hartwell pushed her coffee cup around in her

hands. "It doesn't matter. What matters is that you two overheard that fight. I'm sure you must be thinking about it now."

Mimi simply shrugged. Having a mother-daughter talk with a mother who'd been virtually nonexistent for years was still a novel idea.

"I don't know if you love this young man you were with or not, and I won't pry. I realize I haven't earned that right." Mrs. Hartwell lifted a thin hand as if to reach for Mimi again, then seemed to think better of it and brushed at a strand of hair that had slipped from her chignon. "But I was wrong to say such a thing. It wasn't true."

"You mean, you didn't marry Dad because you were pregnant?"

"No, I mean, yes, we did marry because I was having Hannah. But that wasn't the reason we divorced. It wasn't because of you girls at all."

Tears burned in Mimi's eyes. She'd wanted all her life to believe that she hadn't driven her mother away, but she still didn't quite trust her mother's words. "But you hated the messes I made. All the paint and glitter, and then I brought home that dog and that turtle…"

Her mother reached for her then and took her hand, holding it on the table between them. "I know I complained about all that, honey, but my leaving had nothing to do with you or Hannah or Alison. You have to believe me."

"Then why did you leave?"

Mrs. Hartwell released her hand and Mimi felt as

if she'd been deserted again. She studied her mother as she sipped her drink.

"Because I was immature, irresponsible and self-ish. And frankly I...I wasn't in love with your father. I'm sorry."

Mimi's heart squeezed. Whoever coined the expression "The truth will set you free" forgot to add how much the truth could hurt.

"Not that your father isn't a wonderful man, and he's certainly been a fantastic father, but I was too young when we met, and we just didn't have the kind of passion that keeps a marriage alive. We tried to make it work. Your father tried especially hard, but I was too immature to handle a family." She wiped at a tear in the corner of her eye. "I wish we'd had the right kind of love so you girls wouldn't have been hurt. And, Mimi, I don't want to see you make the same mistake I did. If you want a career, if you want to raise the baby by yourself and wait for Mr. Right, then you should do it."

Mimi frowned. At least her mother was admitting to her mistakes. How could she blame her for leaving a loveless marriage? She couldn't. But she still resented her for leaving her and her sisters. Then again, her mother had been young, foolish, immature. "You really need to tell Hannah all this."

"I intend to, as soon as I leave here."

Mimi nodded, silently conceding that her mother's advice made sense. She still wanted to try out for that soap opera; in fact, the auditions were in less than two weeks.

"But if you've found love with this young man of

yours," she continued. "don't let what happened between your father and me keep you from getting married one day."

Mimi remembered Hannah's comment about her and Seth, that their relationship had been platonic. Hannah and Jake had a fiery, passionate kind of love. Did she and Seth?

They certainly had a passionate chemistry, but was it the everlasting kind of love that could make a marriage work?

SETH SHIFTED in his slacks, trying to get comfortable, the elastic in his new bikini briefs crawling into crevices they weren't meant to find. Tugging at the skimpy underwear, he rang Mimi's doorbell, trying to gain courage.

As soon as he heard footsteps, he brought the bouquet of lilies in front of his face and hid the box of chocolates behind his back. Granted, he looked like the typical clichéd TV hero, but heck, desperate times called for desperate measures.

And he was a desperate man.

The door popped open. "What in the world?"

He dropped his hand so Mimi could see his face. "Hi." The rest of his planned sentence went down the tubes at the sight of Mimi's outfit—a harem costume. Complete with scarf and rings and made of the sheerest fabric he'd ever seen.

"Seth, good grief, what are you wearing?"

"What am *I* wearing?" he croaked. He glanced down stupidly at his own clothes, remembered his shopping trip via the Internet and grinned. "A new shirt. Like it?"

"It looks like you just walked off the plane from Hawaii."

He figured that was a compliment—at least he hadn't been predictable—and tried to formulate his thoughts. Her bare navel was quite a distraction, but he saw her staring at him and wondered if she was still angry. "What about *your* getup?"

"I've been practicing for that audition. The role is a belly dancer."

Images of her belly dancing danced through his head, turning wicked and sexy and… He couldn't go there, not yet. Sex tonight was not part of the plan.

"These are for you. Sorry about the roses." His gaze skated over her body, but he didn't see any red splotches. And she had plenty of skin exposed for him to investigate.

Mimi blushed and motioned for him to come in. "How did you find out?"

He followed her to the foyer. "Hannah stopped by the office."

"I have to tell my family to butt out of my life."

"They love you, Mimi."

"I know, but I can't deal with all this hovering. The next time one of them calls, I'm going to suggest they take a number. Either that or set up a schedule."

He laughed, grateful to see she wasn't as furious as she'd been this morning.

"I'm sorry I offended you earlier."

"Seth—"

"Please listen for a minute."

She leaned against the doorway to the living room, the slinky fabric slipping off one shoulder, grabbing his imagination and taking it for another wild ride, but he quickly reined in his libido. "You probably think I'm a dumb male sometimes, but—"

"You're not dumb, Seth. You're the smartest man I know."

He smiled and gave a small shrug. "Thanks, and I do mean well. But I know we think differently, and I may border on the obsessively organized—"

"That's an understatement."

"Okay, maybe I'm more anal than I thought."

Mimi laughed. "I meant that we think differently."

"Oh, right. Anyway, I realize I upset you, and although I don't totally understand why, because I was honestly just trying to help, I am sorry."

She opened her mouth to protest. "I guess I have been a little sensitive lately."

"Probably hormonal."

She pursed her lips and glared at him.

"I read about it—"

"You and your books."

He ignored her jab. "Give me a chance here, Mimi. I apologized. And I am trying."

"Maybe I am a tad hormonal," she admitted sheepishly. "They say it gets better after the first trimester."

"Whew. I'm looking forward to that."

She swatted him lightly, making her bracelets jangle, and he laughed, forcing himself not to stare at the cleavage the skimpy outfit revealed. But his body couldn't ignore the faint scent of her perfume and the way her breasts jiggled when she moved. Damn. He had to stick to his plan. And it hadn't been to seduce her. At least, not yet.

"I'd say I won't mess up again, Mimi, but I probably will, because I have a protective streak in me when it comes to people I care about." She smiled and his underwear slipped higher into his groin. He shifted, trying to rid himself of the wedgie. "I'd like for us to go to dinner."

"You mean, like a date?"

"Yeah. Could we please start over and have a normal date? Pretend we haven't slept together, that we haven't argued, and that I haven't sent you roses that made you break out in hives or insulted your pride by suggesting I take care of you?"

"What if I said I had other plans?"

"If you meant you're seeing someone else, I guess I'd have to take boxing lessons."

"What if I had to work, to practice for that part?"

He hesitated, sensing this was some sort of test. "I guess I'd have to understand. Or you could dance for me."

"In your dreams."

"Exactly."

Their gazes locked. Tension hummed between them.

"Acting is important to me," Mimi said in a low whisper.

He nodded, grateful he'd gotten to her, at least in some small way. "My job's important to me, too. But people can have jobs and personal lives, too."

Mimi's defenses seemed to soften. She motioned

for him to come into the living room. "All right. Wait here and I'll change."

Mimi's cat darted toward him, and Wrangler hopped off the couch and wobbled his way. Seth nodded. "Fine. I'll wait here. Unless you need help."

"I think I can manage."

"Darn."

Mimi laughed and flitted off down the hall.

Wrangler dove at his pant leg. Seth reached into his pocket for the doggie treat he'd picked up at the pet store on the way over. Point number three on his list—make friends with Mimi's animals. He lowered himself to the floor and held out the treat. His legs were shaking, but he told himself he'd be all right as long as the dog didn't bite his hand off. Instead, it lifted his leg and started to pee on him.

Chapter Fifteen

Mimi quickly slipped off her harem costume. Judging from Seth's wild shirt and jeans, which she'd never seen him in before, he'd planned a casual evening. Odd how his impromptu request had sent a shiver of unexpected excitement skittering though her, pushing her earlier anger to the far recesses of her mind. What had she been angry about, anyway?

She tugged on her jeans, then glanced down in frustration when she had to suck in her tummy to fasten them. She was already gaining weight. In high school, she'd been plump and had worked desperately to tone up her body, but now it was going to pot.

Because Seth's baby was growing inside her.

A tear seeped into her eye, but not a tear of sadness. She lay a hand over her stomach and smiled, for the first time realizing that she was carrying a life inside her. It would be worth it. A boy or girl, maybe with Seth's hair and eyes and his intelligence and... sweetness.

Suddenly anxious to spend the evening with him, she pulled on a dark blue off-the-shoulder sweater and brushed her hair, then hurried to meet Seth.

SETH STOOD UP the moment she entered the room, her cat snuggled in his arms. Mimi's eyes lit with surprise. "You're holding Esmereldo."

"Yeah, am I doing it right?"

Mimi laughed. "She's purring, isn't she?"

He glanced down and nodded. "I think Wrangler and I came to some sort of an agreement." The dog lapped at his brand-new tennis shoes.

"I noticed."

"Are you ready?"

"Yeah. I just need to check on the kittens in the laundry room."

"You have more animals?"

"Temporarily. They were abandoned. I'm keeping them until the vet can find homes for them."

Seth followed her to the laundry room and stared in awe at the five bundles of fur snuggled in the cardboard box. "They're so tiny."

Mimi stroked one of the smallest kittens with a finger. "Someone left the kittens on the stoop at the clinic. They've barely been weaned from their mother."

A fleeting memory pressed into Seth's mind—when he was five, he'd begged for a Labrador puppy, but his parents had refused. He watched Mimi pet each kitten, the affection in her eyes so honest his heart clutched. He couldn't imagine simply abandoning something so small. Just as he couldn't imagine abandoning his own child.

Or his child's mother.

"Do I need to change or am I dressed okay?" Mimi brushed a hand over her jeans.

Seth's gaze surveyed the way the denim molded every delicious curve and inch of her. "No, you look great."

Mimi smiled and he thought of the soft swell of her stomach, which would expand over the next few months. For the first time in his life, he thought that his life might be perfect if he could share it with someone like her.

A FEW MINUTES LATER they parked at the recreational area, and surprise registered on Mimi's face again. He'd considered taking her to a five-star restaurant with tablecloths and fine china and crystal goblets filled with expensive wine. But that would have been predictable. Instead, he'd opted for a night of Putt-Putt at the Crazy Dinosaur Play Center. It had been one of the spots recommended in the book he'd bought on dating.

Minutes later he silently admitted he was having the time of his life. Mimi squealed like a child when she popped her golf ball into the tyranosaur's mouth. "I did it! I got it in one shot! Your turn, Doc."

She'd been calling him Doc all evening, and he'd dubbed her Red. He gauged the distance of the shot, walked the small plank leading to the mouth of the dinosaur, retraced his steps and methodically studied the angles. Laughter sputtered behind him, and Mimi's hand covered her mouth.

"What's so funny?"

"Nothing. I just wondered if you needed a calculator."

He frowned at her teasing tone. "I'm just trying to get a handle on the angle."

"Worried you've got too much power in those muscles?"

Seth's heart raced at the saucy sound of her voice and the wicked glint in her blue eyes. "I can't let myself be bested by a woman."

Mimi winked. "Those are fighting words, Seth."

She was worth fighting for, he decided. He started to tell her so, but the family in front of them turned a curious look their way, and he figured he'd save the comment for a private moment. "I'm glad you warned me. I don't want to step on those feminist toes again." She laughed and he prepared for his shot. One swing and the ball sailed into the pile of sand three feet south of its mark.

Mimi doubled over with laughter. The kids in front of them snickered.

"I thought all doctors played golf," Mimi said.

"Obviously not this one." He trudged to the sand and studied the angle of the ball.

"So what is your game, Seth?"

"I've never played games." His gaze found hers, teasing but loaded with an undercurrent of meaning she couldn't miss.

"Then what's this all about?" She gestured around them.

"I wanted you to see that I'm not totally boring. That I can be unpredictable."

A shocked expression glazed her eyes. Seeing Mimi silent was so rare he raised his iron to swing. "I thought about the drive-in, but I didn't want you to think I was too forward and just wanted your body. Not on our first date.''

Their gazes caught, the irony of what he'd said hitting them both, and they both burst into laughter.

"I don't think you're boring at all," Mimi said softly. "You didn't have to bring me here to prove that."

He swung and missed the ball. She didn't think he was boring? A small improvement…

He suddenly envisioned him and Mimi and a whole brood of kids out for an evening of recreation, Mimi teasing him, his kids teasing him…. Of course, maybe he'd be better at Putt-Putt by then and they'd actually be admiring him, instead.

"Seth?"

"Yeah?"

"Are you all right?"

"Yes."

He took another swing and managed to sink the ball into a comfortable zone for another shot. On the fourth one, he finally hit his mark. She cheered and he kissed her. To his delight, Mimi threw her arms around his neck and kissed him back. Maybe his plan was working.

Seventeen holes later, he threw in the towel with golf. "I guess I proved I'm unpredictable."

"Yes, I don't think I would ever have predicted how bad a golfer you are."

Seth grinned. "Maybe we'll try bowling next time."

Mimi hooked her arm through his. "Did I mention that I bowled on a league in high school?"

Seth curved his arm around her neck. "How about tennis?"

Mimi gave him a thumbs-up. "I was captain of the high-school team."

"Is there any sport you didn't try?"

"Football."

"Very funny." He edged them toward the ice-cream stand.

"Actually I dropped sports for dance and drama. Didn't you play any sports in high school?"

Seth shook his head. "What flavor?"

"Peanut butter chocolate chip."

Seth ordered strawberry and they sat on a park bench, trading tastes of their cones.

"Why didn't you play sports?" Mimi asked. "You sure have the body for it."

Seth raised a brow, automatically sitting straighter. "No time. My folks didn't approve of extracurricular activities."

Mimi frowned and stopped licking her cone. "No fun stuff, huh? Not even art or music?"

Seth shook his head and indicated the ice cream melting down her cone. Mimi did a swipe with her tongue to lap it up. He sucked in a harsh breath, remembering the way she'd used that tongue on him.

"That's sad, Seth. No wonder you're all work and no play."

He shrugged. "My dad said I'd been blessed with intelligence, and I should utilize my brain to its fullest. He sent me to the best schools to obtain an education, not to have fun. He was determined I make a success out of my life."

Mimi thumbed a strand of hair from his forehead. His eyes followed the tender movement, his body aching for more of her touch. "Success means a lot, but so does having friends and fun and...and just laughing."

"I know," he said softly, sincerely. "You make me laugh, Mimi. You make me feel alive."

Mimi wet her lips with her tongue, the ice cream forgotten as they stared into each other's eyes. He gently reached out and pulled her head toward him, flicking his tongue to taste the chocolate ice cream on her lips, the cold flaring into heat as their mouths merged for a slow kiss.

He felt the drip of cold liquid seconds later, then a cold plop. When they finally broke the kiss, he saw the rest of his cone lying in the most precarious spot!

FOUR DAYS LATER, Mimi placed the new low-fat chocolate dessert she'd concocted on the warming tray and scrubbed the counter, grinning as she thought about the past few days. Four days of unpredictability with Seth. First, the Putt-Putt place. Then the zoo, where they'd fed the animals—Seth had even volunteered to be the guinea pig who fed the elephants and had ended up soaked in water and elephant drool. Tuesday he'd taken her to a local storytelling festival, which had proved entertaining and educational. Then last night he'd abducted her from work, waving Dixie Chicks tickets in his hand. She couldn't imagine Seth listening to the female group, but somehow he'd discovered they were her favorite and had finagled two tickets in the second row. She had danced herself into exhaustion, fallen asleep on the way home and he'd carried her inside.

When she'd seen him standing over her bed like some knight in shining armor, she'd almost begged him to make love to her. Almost.

But fear still niggled at her. What if she completely gave her heart to him and he was only pursuing her because of the baby? Would he be able to tolerate living with her less-than-organized manner of house-keeping and her animals? Or would they start to pick at each other until they eventually ended up hating each other?

What if she fell in love with him and the baby got attached to him, then he grew tired of them and left? Would she survive a broken heart? Would their little one be able to bear living without him?

The bell jingled and she glanced at the clock. The lunch rush had just ended, and Penny had left for an afternoon class. Seth entered the café, bringing a burst of sunshine. She couldn't resist a smile, but his parents trailed in behind him, and instantly her nerves went on edge. These people were her baby's grand-parents, she reminded herself. Did they even know about their grandchild?

Judging from the frowns on their faces, Seth might have told them. Of course, they frowned all the time anyway.

"Hi." Seth approached the counter with the sexy grin that turned her inside out. A little voice of fear waved a red flag, and she wondered if it wasn't too late, if she'd already given her heart to Seth and now was just waiting for him to trample it.

"Did you come by to eat?"

Seth leaned on the counter so they could talk more privately while his parents stood back, studying the menu on the chalkboard above them. "We've had lunch. We just stopped by for coffee. My dad wanted to discuss the funding for the support-group sessions. I've brought a ton of research data on divorced couples and single-parent homes to show them."

Mimi winced at the thought of single-parent homes, wondering if she would be added to his statistics next year. "Are your parents going to be there tonight?"

"Yes. Is everything set for the session?"

"Yep. I think the kids will have fun decorating the cookies. And just watch—the parents will enjoy it, too."

"Except for them." Seth gestured toward his own folks. They wore such intense scowls Mimi suspected they were dissecting every item on the menu.

"Do they ever relax and have fun?" Mimi asked.

"Only when they're counting the dividends from their stocks."

Mimi laughed, earning a glare from Seth's mother. Just then the truck driving the billboard advertisement her father had orchestrated drove by. Seth's mother shuddered.

"Seth, can you get that waitress to help us or not?"

Seth raised to his full height. "Her name is Mimi, mother, and we're having a conversation."

"Well, we're ready. We have important matters to discuss." His mother stepped to the counter and ordered a slice of key lime pie. His father ordered black coffee in a haughty tone.

"I'll get a fresh pie from the kitchen," Mimi said. She quickly disappeared into the back.

Seth turned to his mother "Mother, you don't need to be rude."

Seth's father gave him a stern look. "Don't speak to your mother like that. Need I remind you that we're here to discuss funding for your project?"

"I haven't forgotten," Seth said, hating the fact that he had to get their approval. Maybe he should switch to a hospital where his parents didn't have so much influence.

"I can't believe you're friendly with that Hartwell girl. Her father is an embarrassment to the entire town. And look what her sister did to you. Have you lost your mind?"

Seth's hands clenched into fists at his sides. A sharp gasp sounded behind him and he closed his eyes, afraid to look, but already knowing that Mimi had come up behind them and that she'd overheard every word.

MIMI'S HEART SANK. Whether or not the Broadhursts knew about their grandchild or not, they clearly didn't approve of her. She had a feeling nothing would ever change their minds. "Mr. and Mrs. Broadhurst, I realize you were upset about Hannah breaking off with Seth, but my sister didn't mean to hurt him."

"We've been over this before," Seth said in a low voice, aiming a warning look at his folks.

"My father may be flamboyant and a little outrageous with his publicity stunts," Mimi continued, "but he's my father and I love him. I'd appreciate it if you didn't talk about him as if he were a piece of slime you found on your shoe.''

''Young lady, I'll not have you speak to Mrs. Broadhurst so harshly,'' Mr. Broadhurst said. ''You are the hired help here.''

''Well, I never.'' Mrs. Broadhurst fanned her face as if the heat in the room had just been turned up. ''I certainly hope you don't decide to follow in your family's footsteps and embarrass our son like your sister did.''

Mimi clamped her mouth shut, her throat closing as she imagined what their response would be to the news of her pregnant state—her unwed pregnant state.

Seth stepped forward. ''Mother—''

Mimi shook her head at him. ''Don't bother, Seth. The pie's on the house. I hope you enjoy it.'' With a nonchalant shrug, she turned in a flourish of anger, stomped toward the refrigerated section and began to rearrange the already neatly arranged shelves.

Seth came up behind her. ''Mimi, I'm sorry. I'm so embarrassed. My parents were callous and rude.''

She shrugged. ''It's not your fault, Seth. Now go talk to them about the support group. You need that money.''

''I won't ask them now,'' he said. ''I don't want their money or approval.''

Mimi searched Seth's eyes and found concern and regret and some other emotion she thought might be affection…no, love. Suddenly nothing his parents said mattered. ''Go on. I know you don't want to ask for their approval, but your project's worthwhile, Seth. You've worked so hard to help these people and you're making a difference. I see it every time you meet with them. You have to fight for the group or your parents win.''

A slow, tender smile spread over his face. "You really believe in me and my work?''

"Of course I do.'' She squeezed his hand. "Those people need you. Those kids need you. You can't let them down.''

"I'm not going to let my parents win,'' he said in a thick voice. Then he reached up and tucked a strand of hair behind her ear and blew her a kiss that nobody saw but her. And Mimi realized his comment about not letting his parents win referred to something more than the support-group project. She heaved a sigh of relief and forgot all about her earlier outburst. She'd just been given a sign.

But even if he fought for her, for them, was he simply trying to make things work for their baby's sake, or did he really love her?

Chapter Sixteen

Seth winced as the children squealed and chased the kittens. He'd better get used to noise, his own baby would do its share of squealing and crying. And laughing, as long as Mimi was around.

"Shh, let's remember they're just babies," Mimi coaxed softly. "We'll frighten them if we're too loud."

He smiled. Even when Mimi corrected the children, she did it in such a gentle and positive way the kids responded beautifully, avoiding all the power struggles he witnessed in so many disciplinary situations. She gathered the children in a circle on the floor, enclosing the kittens within the group. "Sit very still and let them come to you. Then you can gently pet the kitty's fur. Like this." She demonstrated how to hold out a tentative hand, how to gently rub the kitten's back, stroke between his ears. The children sat, mesmerized, their faces filled with rapture as the kittens found their way into their laps.

Mimi would have homes for the animals before the night was over. Seth frowned, chiding himself for not considering pet therapy before. Just because he'd never been comfortable with four-legged creatures didn't mean he hadn't read about the value of pets with children. Even with adults, he amended, as he watched Georgie's father, Ralph, nestle a tiny calico on his brawny chest. Georgie moved into the crook of his father's arm and hugged his waist.

Twenty minutes later Mimi helped the children settle the kittens in the big cardboard box he'd carried in earlier, instructed them to wash their hands, then directed the parents and kids to the tables where she'd organized the evening's cooking activity. Icing, sprinkles and assorted candies sat in small containers on the table for easy access. Although he hadn't planned on the support group becoming quite so interactive, he hoped Mimi's suggestion worked, especially since his parents had arrived earlier and were looking down their patrician noses.

Ralph appeared no more anxious to participate than his parents, but Nina Simmons, Anita's mother, began singing as she and Anita turned plain sugar cookies into faces that supposedly resembled their own.

"See, I can use the blue icing to make blue eyes like mine," Mrs. Simmons said.

"And I can use the brown candies to make my brown eyes." Anita snatched a handful of the candies and popped two brown ones onto her cookie. "Guess I'll have to eat the blue and orange ones," Anita said with a giggle.

The effects of sugar, Seth thought morosely. He should have warned Mimi the kids would be swinging from the rafters if they kept nibbling on the decorations, but Mimi and the children were having too much fun to point out the potential problems. He'd never seen some of the kids talk so much.

"Look, you can hook them together with icing to make balloons." She drew a line with the pink icing to connect each circle.

"I wanna make a train," Georgie said. "Or a car."

His burly father grunted. "A round car."

"It could be a space car," Georgie said.

"Oh, yeah, I guess it could." Ralph picked up a tube of chocolate icing and drew circles for wheels beneath the cookie.

Georgie squealed. "That's cool, Dad!"

Tough Ralph actually beamed a proud smile and ruffled Georgie's hair.

"I'm making an alien," four-year-old Toby Tucker bellowed. "Like *X-Files*."

"Mine's going to be a snow baby." Laurel picked up a spoonful of vanilla icing and smeared it on her cookies, then added raisin eyes and a carrot slice for a nose.

Seth smiled to himself as the other parents planned their creations. Mimi passed from one child to another, laughing and offering suggestions, encouraging everyone to use their imagination. Finally she saw him watching her and walked over. "What do you think?"

"You've certainly made me rethink my approach. I should be trying more innovative techniques."

Mimi blushed. "You're giving me too much credit. You started this program."

"But you got everyone talking and communicating. You're brilliant, Mimi."

She seemed stunned. "I wouldn't go that far."

"I would." He gently stroked her arm with his fingertips. "I can learn a lot from you about families."

Her eyes glistened with emotion. "Seth, I wish that were true. But I don't even have a degree. And my family was broken, remember."

"It doesn't matter. You're a natural with kids, Mimi. And their parents." He waved a hand around the room. "When I see these moms and dads taking time with their kids, I realize how important the little moments are that build and make a relationship. You may have grown up in a single-parent home, but your dad and sisters obviously had a close loving relationship. Sometimes kids in two-parent homes don't have that closeness."

Mimi leaned against the wooden desk and turned her gaze toward the group. "You're talking about your own family now, aren't you?"

Seth shrugged. "They raised me the way they thought was best. They're just not the touchy-feely type."

She bit down on her lip. "Like my mother. She came to see me the other day."

"Really?" He could see the pain in her eyes.

"She's moving back here, setting up a law office in town."

"How do you feel about that, Mimi?"

Mimi shrugged and picked a sprinkle from her blouse. "It's strange. She's been gone so long I don't feel as if I even know her. And…" She hesitated.

"And what?"

''And she acts like she wants to be friends.'' Mimi turned those big baby-blue eyes toward him. ''But what if we let her back in and she disappears again?''

Seth sucked in a harsh breath at the raw emotion in her eyes. For the first time he felt as if he truly understood Mimi. She was afraid, afraid of being hurt, of being deserted again. Maybe even afraid of love and commitment for the same reason. ''There are no guarantees. I guess you just have to trust your instincts.''

''My instincts get me in a mess sometimes. Look at what happened with Joey, and then...''

''Then me?''

She shook her head, regret clouding her features. ''I didn't mean it like that, Seth.''

''It's okay. I understand, Mimi.'' He covered her hand with his. ''And I won't hurt you. Maybe your instincts are improving. Maybe you learned something from Joey.''

She dropped her gaze from his, biting her lip. ''She wanted to talk about...the pregnancy. Dad told her. Can you believe it?''

Seth thought about his conversation with Wiley. ''How did it go?''

Mimi shrugged, her shoulder brushing his arm. He savored the simple contact, knowing he couldn't touch her in front of all his patients, but he was proud of her, and he desperately wanted everyone to know she belonged with him. A surge of protective feelings swelled inside him.

''She told me not to let her mistakes or her and Dad's divorce keep me from doing what I want.''

His heart pounded. "And what is that?"

Mimi's gaze met his and locked. Tension mounted between them.

"I don't know, Seth. I want to be a good mother."

"You will be, Mimi. Look how wonderful you are with these kids."

"This stuff just comes naturally."

"I told you you have natural mothering instincts. You obviously take after your grandmother."

"Yeah. Speaking of Grammy, I wonder if she might be a little bit psychic."

Ah, the baby blanket and rattle. Seth glanced up and saw his mother frowning in horror at Anita, who had icing smeared from her nose to her toes. Georgie and his dad had their heads bent close, discussing the next phase of their car. Little Laurel suddenly turned with icing-covered hands and darted toward the bathroom, waving her hands in front of her like a white monster. Seth's mother shrieked and backed a good ten feet away as if she was afraid the child might attack her with frosting.

"I hope your grandmother will spend some time with our baby. My mother certainly isn't the grandmotherly type."

Mimi threaded her fingers through his, their hands almost hidden beneath her colorful long skirt. She'd obviously recognized the disappointment in his voice. The intimacy stirred a longing in Seth that was a physical ache. He didn't want to turn out like his parents. Somehow he had to convince Mimi to marry him and save him from the life his parents had planned for him. The life he'd once wanted with all his heart. The life he'd walk away from in a skinny minute if he could have Mimi by his side forever.

THE NEXT DAY, Mimi's stomach quivered as she entered the studio where the new soap *Scandalous* was being filmed. All her life she had dreamed about becoming a star, someone her family would be proud of. Her conversation with Seth the day before replayed in her mind, along with the closeness they'd shared. He'd sounded proud of her ability to work with the kids, as if her lack of a sophisticated job or degree didn't matter. But how could he feel that way when he worked with women like Hannah and that new ER physician, career women who had looks and respect and intelligence? And how would her baby feel about having a waitress for a mother? A nobody, according to Seth's mother.

But would she be a nobody to her child if she loved it and spent time with it? Sure, Seth's parents had prestige and intelligence and respect and careers, but they'd left an emotional void with their own son that no amount of education or money or prestige could fill.

Confusion twisted her nerves and she took a deep breath, reminding herself that this part was a once-in-a-lifetime opportunity, a chance to be recognized, a chance to make it big. She stepped into the auditorium, excitement and anxiety tightening her throat when she spotted the stage and the roomful of other actresses vying for parts on the new show.

A tall female who resembled a Scandinavian goddess and a short man who reminded her of Danny

DeVito occupied front-row seats facing the stage. Another group, five to be exact, holding clipboards and pencils sat beside them—obviously judges. A petite woman dressed in a sharp red suit seemed to be in charge, pointing and telling the various wannabes where to wait.

"I'm Mimi Hartwell." Her bracelets jangled as she spoke. "I came to try out for the belly dancer."

The woman eyed her appreciatively. "Oh, yes, I have your name here. Just sit down. We'll call you shortly."

Mimi smiled and took a seat, studying the other actresses. Some were chatting nervously, others sitting aloof, still others practicing lines.

"Let's start with those reading for the part of the maid."

Mimi's mind wandered while a string of actresses read from the script. She placed her hand over her stomach and thought of the baby lying there. If she did land the part, who would watch the baby while she worked? Hannah? No, Hannah had her own job and a new husband. She would have her own children one day.

Alison? She was busy with her new bridal shop. Day care? A lot of people used day care, although the idea of leaving an infant for long hours didn't seem appealing. Maybe she could hire a nanny to come with her to the studio...but nannies cost money.

An hour later the director had dismissed several candidates for the maid role and two other female characters, and began the belly-dancing routines. Mimi watched in appreciation and trepidation as each actress performed. Two carried off beautiful routines, while one poor girl fell on her face. Another had the coordination of a bat.

"Mimi Hartwell."

"That's me." Mimi jumped up and pasted on a smile, reminding herself to walk gracefully as she climbed the steps to the stage When the music began, she felt the rhythm deep in her soul, and she began to move her hips, soaring through the routine with confidence and skill, envisioning dancing for Seth as she had so many times. When she finished, she saw the pleased smiles on the judges' faces and had a gut feeling she'd gotten the part.

SETH HAD CLEARED his calendar for the day to tie up loose ends. Yesterday he'd felt so close to Mimi. Actually each day they were together, their relationship grew. He no longer thought of Mimi as flashy or impulsive, but fun and sensitive and alive. He no longer simply wanted her in his bed, although he wanted that very badly; he cared about her and wanted her in his life. She would make a wonderful mother.

He sensed that Mimi had grown fond of him, too. Her sweet little touches, the way she said his name, so soft and whispery, and those heated looks that passed between them at the most unexpected times. Like last night, when he'd followed her home. He'd kissed her good-night at the door.

Tonight he'd propose to Mimi again. He thought she was finally seeing things his way—they were two decent, caring, mature people who wanted the best for their child. Although opposites, they had great chemistry and had become friends. They could make this work. Maybe in time they might even learn to love each other.

Feeling optimistic, he'd gone shopping first thing this morning, then cleared out the extra bedroom. After lunch he scrubbed the walls and geared up to paint. He intended to surprise her with the nursery. Since they didn't know the sex of the baby yet, he'd chosen a pale yellow. Hadn't Mimi said once that yellow was her favorite color?

As he rolled on the paint, he thought about the baby store he'd visited that morning and the different kinds of furniture and toys and accessories. He'd splurged on a big blue teddy bear and a silly rocking horse, but he'd forced himself to rein in his impulses before he maxed out his credit card. He didn't want to start marriage strapped for cash.

Finishing everything would take some time and research, he decided. Thank goodness they had eight months. He needed to study consumer reports and compare the brands of furniture, the safety rankings on car seats, read up on toys that provided the most educational value...

Two hours later, proud of his logic and progress with the room, he hurried to shower before he called Mimi. Maybe if he had time first, he'd jump on the Internet and scope out the best deal on baby supplies and diapers. Then he could impress her with all his well-laid plans.

"CONGRATULATIONS, Miss Hartwell, we'd love to have you for the part."

Mimi smiled and shook the short man's hand. Apparently he was the director and had really liked her dancing. "Thank you. I'm delighted."

"I have to tell you, we've had some setbacks, though, and won't be able to begin production until midsummer. Will you be able to work with us then?"

Mimi mentally ticked away the months. Disappointment momentarily blindsided her. "Will you be filming the belly-dancing role then?"

"Probably July. That character doesn't appear in the first few episodes. She's going to start out as a female vixen, but we plan to transform her eventually if she's popular."

"Sounds great." Mimi felt her hopes deflating. "But I'm afraid I won't be able to accept."

The director eyed her over his clipboard. "Oh, dear, but you were so good. Can I ask what the problem is? We really want you, Miss Hartwell. Maybe we can work around it."

Mimi's bracelets jangled as she tucked a strand of hair back into the headdress. "Actually I don't see a way. You see, I just learned I'm pregnant and—"

"Oh, dear, that would be a problem," the woman said.

"A pregnant belly dancer, um, I'm afraid that's not what we pictured," the director said. "Now if your…um, if your situation changes, let us know."

Mimi frowned at his implication, thanked him and headed to her car, her emotions in a tailspin. She'd just gotten the job she'd wanted and lost it in the same day. But it was the director's offhand comment that really irked her. Her situation wasn't about to change, not unless something happened and she lost the baby.

Her knees suddenly felt weak and she clutched the door frame as she climbed into the car. The mere thought of something happening to her child made her ill. She dropped her head forward against the steering wheel and forced herself to take a deep breath, to think positively. She would make sure her baby was well taken care of. After all, even though she'd only known about the baby for a few short weeks, her child had quickly become the most important thing in the world to her. The baby. And Seth.

Chapter Seventeen

Seth stood on Mimi's doorstep, his legs wobbling. He'd done everything he could think of the past few weeks to woo Mimi, everything from changing his underwear to trying to be more impulsive, but what if Mimi said no to his proposal? He couldn't lose her...

He mentally recited the rules for positive thinking he'd used in a recent lecture. Several seconds later Mimi opened the door wearing that sexy harem costume he'd seen once before, a huge bowl of chocolate sauce in her arms, the phone tucked beneath her chin. He saw her body's natural response to the cold outside—a shiver and...

"Hey." She clapped her hand over the receiver's mouthpiece and narrowed her eyes at his dressy shirt and slacks. "Did we have plans?"

"No. But I wanted to see you."

She waved him in, gesturing that she'd try to end the conversation on the phone soon. "Yes, Hannah, I'm fine."

He waited to be attacked by her menagerie of animals, but her cat simply raised a head and looked at him, lowered it again down to finish her nap. Wrangler bounced over to him, wagging his tail. Seth fed the dog the treats, then followed Mimi into the kitchen. A three-layer chocolate dessert, drenched in whipped cream and raspberry sauce identical to the one on that truck advertisement, sat on the counter.

"No, I do not want you to come over, Hannah," Mimi said into the phone. "You have a nice romantic night with your new hubby." Pause. "Yes, and no. I got the part, but they're going to be filming this summer, so I'm out." Another pause. ·

His gut clenched when he realized Mimi was talking about her audition. So she had gotten the part, but couldn't accept it because of the pregnancy? How did she feel about her condition interfering. with her dream?

"Maybe we can have lunch tomorrow or Sunday. Just give me a call."

He sank onto a kitchen chair, his gaze fixed on her as she crossed the room and returned the phone to its base. The sheer fabric of the costume billowed out around her dynamite legs, the overlay of dark purples and other bright colors in the headdress repeated in the fabric covering her breasts. Barely covering her breasts, he amended. They were almost spilling from their thin encasement. His gaze dropped to the tantalizing bare skin below the top. To Mimi's stomach where his baby lay, growing every day. To Mimi's navel, the place he had tasted and tormented with his tongue.

Her gaze sprang to meet his and she licked a glob of chocolate sauce off her finger, her breath hitching.

She saw the hunger in his eyes and mirrored it with her own look of desire. Desire that rocketed through him, hardening his body, tensing every muscle and nerve with the power of it.

"I heard what you said about the part. I'm sorry."

"It's not going to work out."

"Are you okay about it?"

"Yeah." Mimi shrugged and set the bowl on the blue-tile counter near a portable entertainment unit. Her favorite Dixie Chicks CD played in the background. He imagined her dancing around the kitchen, stirring chocolate, the shimmering material whispering across her body as she moved.

The image had lust pooling in his groin. He moved toward her, mesmerized by the flare of excitement he saw in her eyes. "You're not upset?"

"There'll be other parts. Other times," she said softly.

"You can always dance for me," he said, surprising himself at how much he wanted her to do that.

She wagged a finger at him, a hint of mischief sparkling in her eyes. "Don't tell me, you, Seth Broadhurst, doctor of psychiatry, get off on this harem costume."

He had to smile. "Honey, I may be a doctor of psychiatry, but I'm a man first. And any man who saw you in that getup would be turned on." He raised a hand and wiped a drop of raspberry sauce from her chin, then licked it with his tongue.

"You mean any woman wearing this costume would excite you?"

Did he notice a hint of jealousy? "No, not any

woman. Just you." He ran his thumb along her temple, then down her jaw. "Dance for me, Mimi. Please."

She closed her eyes on a feathery sigh and began to move her hips, gyrating slowly, seductively, as the beat of the music slowed and faded into a love song. He touched her as she moved, his breath collecting in his lungs in a painful surge at the way her curves fit beneath his palms, the way her body swayed, the way her breasts rose with every breath she inhaled, the way she threw her head back, uninhibited, daring. His finger drew a soft line down her neck to her breastbone, then dipped to circle a taut nipple beneath the sheer fabric. She arched and groaned, rotating her head slowly, seductively, so he could see the muscles in her throat work as she swallowed. His heart thundered at the scent of her exotic perfume, then stilled when she opened her eyes and reached for his shirt.

His hands dropped to her waist, where he savored the feel of her bare skin while she slowly drew each button from its encasement, taking her slow, sweet time as if performing a striptease for him. Then her hands were inside his shirt, rubbing, stroking, teasing his hard nubs, her hips gyrating into his heat, stroking, tormenting him. She pushed away his shirt and reached for his belt. He sucked in a breath, hoping he didn't lose control as he allowed her to strip off his clothing. Their gazes locked for a moment, resting in surprise on his black briefs. He blushed.

"You are full of surprises, Doc." Her gaze swallowed his burgeoning erection, then lifted to his eyes. "I approve, very much."

He pulled her against him, moaning when her soft heat cradled him. "I want you, Mimi. It feels like it's been forever."

Her hands sank into his hair. "I want you, too, Seth."

He laughed when she squeezed his hips with her thighs, but his voice turned serious when he asked, "We won't hurt the baby?"

She shook her head. "No, Doc. You should know that."

"I've never made love to a pregnant woman before." He cupped her face with his hands and drew her mouth to his for a tender kiss.

"Is that what this is all about?" she asked softly. "Seducing the mother of your child?"

"No." He slowly removed his skimpy underwear, wanting her to see how naked and raw and exposed he felt. "This is because I want you, because I care about you, Mimi. Because I can't stand not being with you."

She drank in his size, the length of his body, the evidence of his need for her and melted into his arms. His hands skated down her sides, searching for buttons or snaps, but Mimi stood back, lifted the top over her head and dropped the flimsy material to the floor. The billowy pants had an elastic waist, so she skimmed them off in seconds. His eyes feasted on bare flesh, the swollen mounds of her breasts arching toward him, taut pink tips begging for his mouth, the kitchen light painting her porcelain skin with a golden glow.

He lifted her onto the yellow-laminate kitchen table, dipped his finger into the raspberry sauce and traced a path over her nipple, then down to her waist, then licked it off, one delicious inch at a time. Mimi writhed beneath him, begging him with her body and hands to ease her torment, but he continued the sensual foreplay by planting kisses from the tips of her toes to the soft folds that cradled her womanhood. Chocolate and raspberry and the tantalizing taste of Mimi filled his senses, and he drove her wild with his mouth and hands, painting her thighs with the sauce and licking it off until she was clawing at him to end the torture. Finally he parted her legs, looked into her eyes and smiled, then dipped his head and drank deeper, refusing to take her until he'd tasted her release.

And when he did, the sweet heady taste drove him wild. He was like a starving animal as he pushed into her, pumping and grinding their bodies together with an intensity he'd never imagined, channeling all his emotions into giving her pleasure. And when she cried out his name and clutched his back, winding her legs around his waist, her body rippled with waves of ecstasy. He groaned her name and drifted to the clouds with her. And in his heart, he knew he'd just made her his forever.

MIMI HAD NEVER felt so peaceful and loved and sated. She drifted into a blissful sleep and dreamed about Seth and love and sex and babies and a wedding in the gazebo on her grandmother's property on Pine Mountain with her entire family, even her mother, in attendance. When she awoke in Seth's arms, she half feared the night had been just a dream, but his warm, tender smile caressed her and his arms cradled her tightly.

"How about some breakfast and a shower, then we go to my place for a while?"

Mimi searched his face. "Your place?"

"Yes." He dropped a kiss on her nose. "I have a surprise for you."

"You do? More wild underwear? Leather, maybe?"

He threw back his head and laughed, a deep, sexy rumble that sounded so masculine Mimi imagined waking up to it every morning. "As a matter of fact, I do. I'll even give you a fashion show if you want, but I have another surprise."

Mimi tossed the covers back, revealing their naked bodies, rosy in the aftermath of love. "Race you to the shower."

Seth chased after her, and Mimi found herself in deep lust again when she saw the spray of water cascading across his muscular chest and corded thighs. Temptation won again and she twined her arms around him, kissed him senseless and climbed in his arms for a wild morning ride. Several minutes later they finally bathed and left the shower.

"I'll throw together some breakfast while you get dressed," Seth whispered against her neck.

Mimi luxuriated in the offer and dressed in a casual blue shirt and jeans, wincing when the zipper once again hesitated over the small bulge of her stomach. She would have to resort to wearing looser clothing soon, she realized. Maybe even visit that store Seth had found. Surprised that the idea of maternity clothes didn't bother her as it once had, she went in search of Seth and food.

SETH'S HANDS trembled as he clasped Mimi's fingers and dropped to the soft gray carpet in his bedroom. He'd just given Mimi a tour of his house, except for the nursery, which he wanted to save until their engagement was official. Then he wanted to end the tour with a mind-boggling kiss and a romp in his bed. But first things first. He pulled out a velvet ring box, lifted a diamond ring and slipped it on her finger. "Mimi, I want us to get married."

Mimi stared openmouthed at him. "Oh, my goodness. Is this…your surprise?"

"Well, no. I mean, yes, sort of."

"Seth…"

"Shh. Just listen. I have everything worked out. We can get married right away and you can move in here. That's why I wanted to show you the house today. So what do you think? Because if you don't like the house, we can sell it and get something more contemporary, more modern, more…more whatever you want." She shot an odd look at the Chippendale love seat, and he realized he was rambling, but Mimi still hadn't replied, and her stunned expression didn't look optimistic. "It's just a house to me."

"It's a lovely house, Seth. A little formal, but lovely."

"It'll be a home with you and our baby here."

Mimi's eyes filled with tears. Happy or sad? He still couldn't completely read her.

"Don't cry, sweetheart. Everything's going to be fine. I have everything planned." He grabbed her hand and dragged her to the nursery. "We need to get married soon before...well, we both want what's best for the baby, and that's us together. See, I've already started a nursery. I thought you liked yellow, but I waited to choose the rest of the decor until you were here." He smiled, proud of his planning. "I have several furniture catalogs, and I'm researching the safest kind of car seats—"

"Car seats?"

"Yes, you have to know which kind to buy. And we need a playpen and educational toys and..." He was babbling again. God, what this woman did to him. "What do you think of the room?"

Mimi's gaze traveled the pale yellow walls. "It's nice. But I haven't even thought about furniture or a baby's room."

"Oh, we have plenty of time, but I thought I'd get the ball rolling. Plus, it'll take a while for me to check all the consumer reports, do some comparison shopping."

The doorbell rang and Seth frowned and checked his watch. "I wonder who's stopping by so early."

The bell chimed again. "You'd better go see who it is, Seth."

"All right. You wait here and think about the room and what kind of furniture you'd like while I get rid of whoever's there."

Mimi nodded, and a slight moment of anxiety attacked him. She still hadn't said yes to his proposal, he realized as he raced for the door.

MIMI STARED at the teardrop diamond glittering on her finger, then the spacious room painted her favorite color, and the stack of consumer reports and furniture catalogs. She felt so overwhelmed a lump lodged in her throat. She did love Seth, she could no longer deny it, yet he still had never used the L-word. Although, he had shown her he cared—he'd tried to be impulsive in planning their dates, he'd even bought new underwear and that ridiculous Hawaiian shirt, and had made friends with her animals. He must love her. Surely he wouldn't go to this much trouble if he was only acting out of a sense of responsibility.

Her gaze rested on a big teddy bear perched on a blue-and-yellow wooden rocking horse, making the room come alive and look playful, something she would never have imagined Seth choosing. But that stack of catalogs in the corner of the floor mocked her, screaming out the differences between the two of them.

Seth was so prepared, already planning and thinking of everything, while she felt at a loss, like a failure because she hadn't thought of anything the baby would need. She'd been too busy thinking about herself and the changes in her life and the audition and now…what kind of career she would have. Would she continue managing the café for the rest of her life? Quit work and become Seth's wife? Jump from letting Hannah and her father take care of her to letting Seth?

Shaken by the thought, she tiptoed to the doorway, heard Seth's parents' voices in the foyer and decided to stay out of sight. Taking a deep breath, she stepped back into Seth's bedroom, trying to picture herself living in this house. Lying in his bed at night, sharing the bathroom, raising their child here, her things scattered around... Would her disorganization drive Seth crazy?

The house was spacious, with lots of windows and natural light, and if she added a few splashes of color here and there and got rid of some of his uncomfortable furniture, especially that hideous pea-green love seat, it could be extraordinary. Her gaze fell on a stack of books beside Seth's bed, and she walked over to examine them, half expecting some psychology textbooks. Odd. Instead, a book on dating topped the pile. Curious, she thumbed through the book. Her pulse jumped. Certain sections had been highlighted in yellow.

Favorite Dates. For a fun, innovative change, try an evening of Putt-Putt golf. Surprise your girl with tickets to her favorite concert. Take her to the zoo.

The dates listed were the same as the days Seth had arranged their outings—spontaneous, huh?

Seth's laptop stood open on the desk. Curious, she glanced at the screen and saw the title of his entry— Every Baby Needs a Daddy. Plan to Win Mimi. Her breath stalled in her lungs. The first paragraph described his desire to raise his baby and be a part of its life. He'd even scribbled notes—advice from Wiley? Her father had talked to Seth? What had he done? Threatened him with a shotgun if he didn't marry her? Anger and hurt welled up in her chest.

She searched the folder for any sign that Seth really wanted *her,* any note that he loved her and hadn't been strong-armed by her father or acting out of his sense of responsibility, but no. He'd very methodically and carefully outlined a plan to win her affection, detailing each date, when to send flowers, when he should spring the proposal. It was nothing more than a business plan.

Mimi's heart thundered with fury. Seth hadn't fallen in love with her at all. The big lug had formulated a well-ordered plan to sucker her in so he could gain access to his baby. *He* should have been the actor, not her. And she'd fallen for every ploy. Even worse, she'd fallen in love with him!

She was so angry she was shaking. Uncaring now whether his parents were privy to her relationship with Seth, she stomped into the foyer.

"Mimi?" Seth looked agitated, as if he'd been arguing with his parents.

"Miss Hartwell, what are you doing here?" Mr. Broadhurst asked.

Mrs. Broadhurst smiled a brittle smile. "Yes, it's a little early, isn't it?"

"I—"

"My parents and I were discussing the funding for the support group," Seth said, cutting her off. He pulled her toward him, and draped his arm around her shoulders. "And Mimi's here because I invited her. Father, Mother, Mimi and I are getting married."

"What?" Mrs. Broadhurst brought a hand to her

forehead as if she might faint. "She would be an embarrassment to the family."

"You can forget the money for the support group if you marry *her*," Mr. Broadhurst snarled.

Mimi decided to save the project and save Seth's mother from any more theatrics. Besides, family was everything, and she'd never forgive herself if she came between Seth and his parents. She would never fit in with them, either. "Don't worry, Mr. and Mrs. Broadhurst, your son is mistaken." She turned to Seth, her heart breaking. "Seth, we'll work out some kind of shared custody for the baby, but—"

"The baby!" Mrs. Broadhurst screeched.

"Good Lord, son, you haven't…" Mr. Broadhurst swiped at his forehead.

Mimi tossed Seth's ring at him, along with the book on dating and a copy of the computer notes. The words he'd written about her father taunted her— "Wiley convinced me that I need to be part of my child's life."

"We're not getting married. Ever."

"But, Mimi, I thought you were starting to care for me."

"Remember, Seth, I'm an actress." Mimi grabbed his car keys, slammed out of the house and climbed into his car, not caring if he reported it stolen. It would be just one more charge to add to the charge she'd be slapped with once she finished with her meddling father.

Chapter Eighteen

Seth's first instinct was to run after Mimi, but she'd taken his car, so he was virtually stranded with his parents. And she'd only been *acting?* But why?

Because he'd kept reminding her that they were responsible people who should do what was right for the baby. He'd basically guilted her into trying to make a relationship work.

A relationship she'd made clear she didn't want.

"At least the girl is showing some sense," his mother said, digging the knife into his bleeding heart even deeper. "She knows she won't fit into our lifestyle. And heaven forbid—we'd have to invite her father to the club!"

"Have you discussed alternatives to this pregnancy?" his father asked.

Seth stared at his parents, appalled. His stomach churned at his father's insensitive, uncaring suggestion. This was his grandchild he was discussing, as if the baby were nothing but a bad investment he could dump without reservation.

"Mother, I can't believe you pride yourself on

good manners and etiquette when you are so rude and arrogant."

His mother gasped and clutched her chest.

He glared at his father. "And I can't believe you'd even hint that I would think of an 'alternative.' Then again, from the example you two set as parents, I shouldn't be surprised. At least Wiley Hartwell loves his daughters and isn't afraid to show it."

"Son, I don't know what that tramp did to you," his father said, "but you're thinking with your lower anatomy now, not your brain. When a little time has passed, you'll see we're right."

Seth stabbed at his father with his finger, fury in every word. "I will never think you're right. I love that woman and I intend to marry her." Her words knifed through him again, the pain still raw. "If my friends don't like it, then I'll find new ones." He lowered his voice to a lethal tone. "And if you or your friends don't like it, then I don't need you in my life. And neither will your grandchild."

"But you can't even be sure this baby is yours!"

"That's right," his father said smugly. "Have you asked for paternity tests? The girl may just be after your money."

Seth seethed. "The baby's mine. I don't have to ask her because I know." He jabbed his father in the chest again, grinding out every word. "And don't you ever insinuate anything so vile about the woman I love again." He hesitated when he realized what he'd just said. It was true. He loved Mimi. He just hadn't been able to tell her. His father started to speak, but he cut him off, his tone lethal. "Mimi is not the one who's obsessed with money—you two are."

His mother gaped. "Well, I never!"

His father's nostrils flared. "You'll regret this decision one day. Then you'll come crawling back to us."

Seth forced a smile and pointed to the door, indicating he wanted his parents to leave. "The only thing I regret is that I didn't marry Mimi Hartwell sooner."

And that I didn't succeed in making her fall in love with me.

HELL HAD NO FURY like Mimi Hartwell on the warpath. She barreled into her father's office, ignoring the shocked looks of two of his salespeople. Her heart ached so badly, it had become a physical pain shooting all the way through her. "I have a bone to pick with you, Dad."

Wiley's ruddy skin turned as red as his bright crimson jacket. He flapped his hands, signaling his sales staff to leave. "I believe we can talk later, folks."

The man and woman rushed out, stumbling over each other in their haste, leaving Mimi and her father alone. She tapped her acrylic nails on her father's desk. "I cannot believe you interfered in my life like that."

"L-like what?" Wiley stuttered.

"You went over to Seth's and tried to strong-arm him into marrying me."

Her father held up a hand as she stalked toward him. "Wait, Mimi, it's not what you think."

Mimi picked up a glass paperweight from his desk.

Wiley backed farther into the corner, looking afraid she might hit him with it. "So, you're telling me you didn't go to Seth's after you found out about the baby?"

"Well…uh…yes, I went to see him."

"And you talked about me and marriage?"

Wiley shifted sideways, clutching the lapels of his jacket as if to protect himself from her anger. "Uh, yes, we talked about you and him and…um, that you two should get married."

"Oh, you think we should?"

"Of course I think you should."

"Because I'm pregnant, right?"

"Can you think of a better reason?"

"Yes! Being pregnant is the worst reason to get married. Look at you and Mom."

"Honey, I told you your situation is different. Didn't your mother come by and talk to you?"

"Yes," Mimi exploded, "and don't think you're getting away with that one, either. How dare you tell Mom my secret without consulting me!"

"She cares about you, honey. She's your mother."

"She hasn't been around enough to care."

"But she's a woman and she understands this pregnancy thing better than me. I've always tried to be there for you girls, but when you went through puberty and all…" He paused, wiping a drop of sweat from his forehead, then continued, "Sometimes I felt you needed a woman's ear."

Mimi's heart squeezed. "Dad, you…you've been wonderful." Seth's note ran through her mind. *Every baby needs a daddy*. Seth would make a wonderful father, too.

"And just because people mess up and don't always do things the way we want them to doesn't mean they don't care." Wiley tried to placate her with his calm voice, the one he always used when he thought her an hysterical teenager. "You don't want to marry Seth?"

"Of course I do! That's not the problem."

Wiley scratched his head, sending his springy hair into wild disarray. "I'm sorry, honey, but I'm not following."

Mimi dropped into the chair beside her father's desk. The vinyl screeched beneath her as she squeezed the edges. "Dad, don't you get it? I don't want Seth to marry me because he *should*. I want him to marry me because he *wants* to."

THE NEXT WEEK was hell.

Seth hadn't eaten or slept and had barely dragged himself to work each day, slogging through his therapy sessions with his patients like a robot. Everywhere he went, everything he saw, reminded him of Mimi. And the family he had lost—not his parents, but Mimi and his child. On the way home, he'd gone to a drive-through hamburger joint and gotten all lump-throated at the sight of a bunch of kids playing on the outdoor playset. And yesterday he'd nearly broken down when Ralph had told him he was taking Georgie to a Braves game.

Would he ever get to take *his* child to a ball game? Teach him or her how to swim?

Would he ever hold Mimi in his arms again? Hear her soft laughter? Feel the energy and excitement for life he felt at her simplest touch?

His head throbbed from worry, his chest ached with loneliness. Hell, he'd never been lonely in his life. He actually used to enjoy being alone; now he hated it. He paced the floor of the unfinished nursery, wondering what to do. He loved Mimi. Desperately, infinitely, soulfully loved her. With all his heart.

Only he'd discovered too late—after she'd walked out the door.

He wrung his hands. He had to figure out where his plan had gone wrong so he could come up with a better one. All week he'd contemplated the theory that Mimi didn't love him or find him attractive, but their recent bout of lovemaking and the way she'd cried his name in ecstasy made him wonder. She couldn't have been that good an actress, could she?

No.

Feeling better, he considered other possibilities. Should he go back to the dating book, the Mars-Venus theory, the book on stages of pregnancy?

An engine rumbled and died outside in the driveway, and he jumped. Already agitated, he decided if it was his parents, he'd simply refuse to open the door.

He peeked through the window and saw the whole Hartwell gang emerge from a silver Suburban, one of Wiley's weekly specials he recognized from his latest ad. He shuddered as Wiley, Alison, Hannah and her new husband marched single file up his drive looking like bounty hunters. He was obviously the prey. Why had they brought Hannah's husband? In case they needed some muscle?

A fleeting idea crossed his mind—he could pretend he wasn't home. After all, his car was missing from the driveway. Then again, he'd faced his family's wrath, so what the hell, he could take on the Hartwells. Although Jake did have about two inches and thirty pounds on him.

Deciding death by the Hartwells might be better than life without Mimi, he swung open the door before the bell even rang. "I guess I should have been expecting you."

The foursome strode in, looking somber and angry as they congregated in his den.

"I suppose Mimi talked to you."

Wiley rubbed the back of his neck, looking chagrined. "Well, I'd say she talked *at* me. Didn't much like my interference."

"We waited all week, hoping you and Mimi would work things out," Alison said.

"I don't know how." Seth realized he sounded pathetic. He was supposed to be the shrink, the one with the answers, yet he didn't have a clue.

Wiley shrugged. "We're talking about my baby girl here and her future."

"And our sister and niece," Alison said. "Or nephew."

"It's important," Hannah said. "Grammy Rose wanted to come, but we didn't have time to go get her."

Seth turned to Jake with a curious look.

"I'm here as a referee, just in case," Jake said with

a twitch of a grin that made Seth relax slightly. At least he had an ally of sorts—Jake hadn't come to stomp on his face. He'd obviously suffered the skepticism of the Hartwell gang before.

"So what exactly happened with Mimi?" Hannah asked.

"Yeah, she's been miserable all week." Alison stalked toward him. "Crying her heart out."

"What?" Hope bubbled inside him.

Hannah arched a brow. "You think that's something to smile about?"

Wiley stepped forward, his hands fisted.

"No, I… It just gives me hope. I didn't think she cared."

"She's in love with you, you big buffoon," Alison said.

He glanced at Hannah for confirmation. Her other eyebrow shot up. "Tell us your side."

Seth shifted and jammed his hands into his pockets. "Everything seemed to be going fine until that morning I showed her the nursery."

"You've already fixed a nursery?" Alison asked.

"Well, not all the way," Seth explained. "But I have catalogs on furniture and supplies, and I'm researching the best kind of car seats."

Hannah rolled her eyes. Jake took a seat and folded his big arms as if settling in for a show.

"Safety's important," Seth protested. "I want our baby to have the best, and it takes time to study consumer reports."

Alison shook her head. Wiley rubbed his neck again. Hannah pressed a hand to her temple. "Forget the consumer reports. Tell us what you said when you proposed.''

Seth chewed the inside of his cheek, feeling more exposed than he had in those ridiculous bikini briefs.

"Word for word," Alison ordered.

Seth searched his memory. "I...I told her I wanted us to get married. That I had everything planned, that we could live here or move if she wanted, then I showed her the baby's room."

Alison gave him a sympathetic look. Wiley clucked. Jake spread his big hands on the chair ends and shook his head.

"What? What's wrong with that? I took her on a date every night. I even bought books on romance and highlighted things to do. But in the end, she didn't want me."

"How can men be such idiots?". Alison said.

Hannah silenced her by slicing her hand through the air. "I just have three words for you, Seth, and I want you to listen carefully."

He closed his mouth. He supposed he could use some advice.

"I love you."

"What?" Hannah loved him? What about her husband?

She repeated the words, slowly, as if he were a child. "I love you."

He stabbed his thumb into his chest, his knees shaking. "You love me? But...but it's too late for us, Hannah. Like you said, we're just friends. I love Mimi now and our baby." He chanced a panicked glance at Jake, expecting him to leap up and kill him any second. "And what about him?"

Hannah rolled her eyes again. Alison and Wiley looked at him as if he was stupid. Jake actually chuckled.

"I don't mean I love you, Seth. I mean, that's what you should have told Mimi."

"But I...I did."

"You said those words?" Alison asked.

Seth thought back to every thing he'd done to win Mimi. The dates, the flowers, the great sex, the planning of the baby's room. "I...I guess I never actually said the words. I showed her, though. I thought that was enough."

Hannah smiled sympathetically. "Sorry, Seth, it's not enough. Women want the words."

Alison nodded. Wiley and Jake looked glum, but they nodded as well.

Seth bobbed his head. "All right. I'll call her."

The Hartwell clan shook their heads in unison.

"Not good enough?"

"Nope. You'll have to do it in person," Alison said.

"Yeah, and it may take some doing to convince her, since you botched it the first time," Hannah said, a trace of disgust in her voice.

"I wish I'd read a book on this," Seth grumbled.

"You and your books," Hannah said.

"Maybe you should try being a little more spontaneous," Alison suggested.

"I did. I took her somewhere different on all our dates and bought new clothes. I even..." No, he would not admit to buying that underwear. "I even bought treats for her dog."

Hannah pointed to the highlighted sections in the dating book. "You took her to these places, right?"

Seth nodded, feeling lost. "I said I tried being spontaneous. I'm not very good at it."

"He sounds hopeless," Alison added with a frown.

"Cut the man some slack." Jake stood and patted his shoulder in a show of male solidarity. "You learn as you go, man. Take a pointer from a detective. Next time you make a plan, don't write it down. Paper trail—leaves evidence."

"What did you do?" Seth asked. "To win Hannah, I mean."

Jake blushed and ducked his head. "I bought her a bride doll."

Seth frowned in thought. "You think Mimi would like a bride doll?"

"No," Hannah and Alison both said at once.

"Hannah collects dolls," Jake clarified. "And it had to do with that hope chest."

"Ahh." Mimi had received baby things in her hope chest, and he'd already tried that route with the maternity clothes. Not exactly romantic. But he'd wanted to prove he'd be a good father. He suddenly had an epiphany. What about showing her that he would be a good husband?

His parents had given him the monetary things, the education, but never the love, the affection. Had he been doing the same thing with Mimi? Committing his house, his money, but not his heart?

Jeez. He sank onto the sofa and lowered his head

into his hands. Defeat settled over him. How could he prove his love?

Mimi didn't collect dolls. And he certainly hadn't had a role model for a loving relationship. His parents were about as loving as tree stumps.

Alison slipped a business card from her wallet. "When you convince her, Seth, I want you and Mimi to be my first customers." He read the name of her bridal shop and nodded.

"I have to talk to her."

"Won't do any good now," Wiley mumbled.

"Why not? I won't let myself believe it's too late."

Hannah smiled. "That's the spirit."

"She's driving to Grammy Rose's for the night," Alison said. "She was packing the Miata when I drove by."

Wiley clucked his teeth. "I've got to talk to Mimi about that little Miata."

"I was thinking the same thing. It's not safe for a baby, is it?" Seth asked.

"You're not taking Mimi's sports car away from her," Alison said.

Wiley looked chagrined again. He slung an arm around Seth. "All right. She can keep the Miata, but you'll need a good family vehicle, too. Listen, son— I can call you son, right?"

"Well, yeah, sure."

"Good, about time we got some men in this family to even things out." Wiley laughed. "Now, I can cut you a good deal on a Cadillac SUV. It's a real beaut, sportylike, got less than ten thousand miles. Been driven by this little old lady from Hopewell, just drove it around town. Never even taken it on the highway…''

MIMI BLINKED BACK another onset of tears. She'd never been more miserable in her life than she'd been this week. Damn Seth for taking her out and letting her get used to him.

For making her fall in love with him.

She finished packing her car for an overnight trip to her grandmother's when she noticed the message light blinking on her answering machine. She wondered if Seth had called and hurriedly stabbed the button.

''Miss Hartwell, this is Don Wagner, the director of *Scandalous,* calling. We were so disappointed you couldn't join our show and really want some local talent in the production. So we discussed several possibilities and have an offer for you. We're writing a vixen redhead named Cassandra into the show and think you'll be perfect for the part. You have the face and the talent. She's going to be a pregnant stripper who slept with her best friend's boyfriend. When she has the baby, her friend kidnaps it. I won't go into all the scenarios, but we'd like you to come in Monday and discuss the details.''

Mimi's head spun as the message wound down. The director listed his phone number and gave her another wave of compliments before he hung up. The realization that she'd just been offered a lead role in the show, an even bigger part than the one she'd originally auditioned for, filtered through her brain and she felt like shouting. She couldn't wait to tell her family. To tell Seth.

No, she wouldn't be running to Seth.

Confusion filled her. Here was the chance she'd wanted, the chance to make it big. And she could use the income to help raise her baby.

She sank onto the bed. Only, the part sounded as if it would take a lot of hours, and although the character sounded fun, she also sounded a little seedy. Other reservations kicked in, and her gaze fell on the hope chest at the foot of her bed. Why didn't she feel as excited as she'd expected? Who would take care of her baby when she was filming? Although she dearly loved her dad and his wacky advertisements, sometimes she and Hannah and Alison had been slightly embarrassed by some of his outlandish publicity stunts. Some actresses actually got slated as really being like the characters they portrayed. How would her child feel when he saw her acting as a stripper on a show entitled *Scandalous?*

Chapter Nineteen

Sunday crawled by for Seth. He itched to finish the nursery, but he decided to wait until he and Mimi could pick out the rest of the room's decor together. That is, if she agreed to marry him.

Insecurities stabbed at him, and he wondered momentarily if he would be forever messing up with her, disappointing her in some way. But his life felt empty without her, the colorless walls in his house like a mausoleum. He had never fully understood depression, except in a clinical way, but if how he'd felt the past week and a half without Mimi was any indication, he now had an inkling of its power. There was a whole lot more to life and dealing with people than what was written in books. He'd take Jake's advice on marriage—learn as he went.

And pray his knees didn't wear out from scraping them on the ground every time he knelt to beg forgiveness. With Mimi, he had a feeling it would be often. He just prayed he could make her love him one day.

He thumbed through the Sunday paper, reading the business section and stock reports, but he dropped the paper and various sections scattered. His gaze landed on the Pets section and he had a brainstorm. Mimi didn't collect dolls, but she did collect animals.

He grabbed the insert and began to scan the contents.

MIMI LEANED BACK in the porch swing beside her grandmother and smiled as the two of them flipped through the old photo albums, her grandmother regaling her with tale after tale of family members, including escapades from her own childhood. Mimi savored the stories and her grandmother's wit while she logged the stories in her mind to pass on to her own children.

"This is the day each of you girls were born." Grammy Rose pointed to photos of Hannah and Alison and Mimi's birth pictures. Mimi stared at the photo, one hand covering her stomach. Would her baby resemble her? Seth? Would their child spend one Christmas with her, the next with Seth? One birthday at one house, the next year... And what if Seth moved on and married someone else? What if his wife didn't want their baby?

"And here's your first birthday party. You entertained everyone with a little jig and you'd barely learned to walk. Then when you were two, you made mustard handprints on the walls for an art show."

Mimi laughed, wondering if her own child would possess her creative spark. If so, she'd warn Seth— for his weekends with the baby.

"And when you were five, you put on a magic show. Pulled a real live turtle out of a hat."

Mimi noticed the frown on Hannah's face as she stood in the background. "Did Hannah always look so sad?"

Her grandmother's smile faded. "She was a quiet one, always kept things to herself, studied all the time. But you...mercy, you were born chattering."

"I always admired Hannah," Mimi admitted. "I wanted to be more like her."

Grammy Rose curled a gnarled hand around Mimi's. "Yes, Hannah is special, but so are you in your very own way. We all have our gifts, Mimi." Tears glistened in her grandmother's gray eyes. "Appreciate who you are. You were always the one who made us laugh, who brought joy into our lives with your vibrant smile."

Mimi remembered her grandmother's letter from the hope chest.

"But you also had the most compassion for people and for animals. And I believe you're the one meant to carry on the family stories."

"I'd love to do that," Mimi said, touched. She glanced through the album, smiling at the pictures of their father with them, her heart tugging at the obvious absence of photos of her mother. She didn't want her child to look at an album one day and feel that same absence of a parent. If she took the acting job, she'd be working long hours, maybe traveling a lot. She might even miss some of the important moments in her child's life. Like the first time she walked or talked.

She wanted to be the kind of mother she'd wanted

as a child, the type she'd never had. She wanted her child to admire her.

Grammy tucked a loose curl behind Mimi's ear. "I know you didn't drive all the way up here to see me just to look at old photographs. Talk to me, hon."

Mimi smiled. "Did Dad or Hannah tell you about me and Seth and the baby?"

Grammy nodded, her solemn eyes full of wisdom. "You have a lot on your plate right now. What can I do to help?"

"I'm confused, Gram."

"Do you love Seth, honey?

Mimi swallowed, her heart squeezing. "Well, yes, I love him, but…"

"But you're afraid."

Mimi swallowed, tracing her hand around the edges of the photo album.

"Do you think your young man loves you?"

"I don't know. I think so, but his feelings are all so tangled up with the baby."

"That's the way families are, you know. Once you bring a child into it, the love is all tangled together. But just because you and Seth came at your relationship a little backward doesn't mean it can't be true love."

Mimi nodded. "What if I disappoint him, though? His family thinks we're wrong for each other, that I'll embarrass him because I'm not a doctor or a professional."

The age spots on Grammy Rose's hands darkened in the afternoon sunlight slanting through the porch trellis. "If they feel that way, that's their problem, not yours. Be proud of who you are, then others will see that pride and love you the same way.''

Maybe that was *her* problem, Mimi realized. It wasn't that Seth didn't love her, it was that she had never loved herself the way she should. She'd blamed herself when her mother left and tried to overcompensate for all the sadness in the house by joking around, but she'd never forgiven herself. And she'd compared herself to Hannah, which was ridiculous. There were all kinds of people in the world, one type no better than another. The differences sometimes complemented each other.

Just as she and Seth would complement each other. They would each bring different things to their child and to a marriage. Seth's words echoed in her mind. *You make me feel alive.* And he made her feel complete.

''Grammy, when you gave me the hope chest, did you have some kind of premonition that I would end up pregnant?''

Grammy smiled. ''Heavens no, hon. I just knew you were a natural mother, that's all.'' She urged Mimi to stand. ''Come on, let's finish this talk while we try my new recipe.''

''Is it low-fat, Gram?'' Mimi patted her slightly swollen stomach. ''I do have to watch the weight, you know.''

Grammy chortled. ''Pshaw. You're eating for two now. I say that baby needs a healthy dose of my pecan praline fudge cake.''

Mimi followed her grandmother into the kitchen.

She could already feel the pounds rolling onto her hips.

"You know," Grammy said as she pulled out ingredients from her old-fashioned pie safe. "I wish that little teahouse was still open. Remember the one down in Pine Hollow we used to go to when you were little?"

Mimi placed the eggs on her grandmother's battered wooden work surface. "Yes, the one where the kids put on shows. I got up and sang *Mary Poppins* songs."

"That's the one. We used to have so much fun there on Sunday afternoons. I wish there was some place like that around. I'd love to take the baby when she gets bigger."

"She?" Mimi narrowed her eyes at her grandmother. "Are you psychic, Grammy?"

"No, that was just a figure of speech. Reckon I'm so used to having granddaughters I don't think in terms of boys."

Mimi laughed.

"Anyway, I tried to get your cousin Rebecca interested, but she wants to open a bookstore in Sugar Hill."

Mimi froze, one hand on the box of cocoa, an idea forming in her mind. Yes, that was the answer. It would be perfect. She rushed over and hugged her grandmother. "Oh, Grammy, you're brilliant."

Grammy Rose looked stunned. "Mercy, child, what did I do?"

"I'll explain later." Mimi tossed her apron on the

counter. "Do you mind if I make a couple of phone calls before we get started?"

Grammy shook her head, then Mimi went to set her plan in motion. Once she worked things out, she intended to have a long talk with Seth.

MONDAY MORNING Seth knocked on Mimi's door, ready to set his plan in motion. He'd written it all out the night before, then burned the papers in the fireplace, so he wouldn't leave a trace of evidence. It was the best he could do at being spontaneous.

He rang again, praying Mimi hadn't totally given up on him and had decided to avoid him altogether. Finally he heard footsteps, then the door inched open. She looked half-asleep, her wild hair tousled, a satiny robe clutched to her chin.

"Seth?"

"I came to give you this." He knelt and picked up the box of squirming puppies. The homely little mutts had kept him up all night with their crying. He'd told himself it was good practice for when the baby came, all those night feedings.

Mimi stared at them, then at him, dumbfounded. "You brought me puppies?"

"Yes, because I love you."

Her eyes widened. "What did you say?"

"I said I love you, Mimi Hartwell." Then he brushed her lips with his, turned and sauntered away.

He heard Mimi yell behind him, "You know I can't possibly keep them all."

"We'll find them good homes!" he called back just before he climbed into his car and drove away.

SETH HAD SAID he loved her.

What the hell was the man up to? Was this another plan he'd devised on his computer? Dropping a batch of homeless puppies off and saying he loved her, then walking away? Of all the infuriating, sneaky, *wonderful* things to do…and he'd said *we'll* find them homes, as if he planned to help her.

He'd also said he loved her. He'd actually said it. Then why had he left?

The puppies yelped and jumped against the box, peeing and screeching and whining. They were undoubtedly the ugliest little creatures she'd ever seen, some kind of cross between a rat terrier and a boxer, with small round faces and wiry hair and stubby toes.

"You're adorable," Mimi cooed as she cuddled them in her lap. Her mind raced over the plans for the day. How the heck was she supposed to finish the details on her new venture with four little babies who needed her? And with the memory of Seth's parting words still fresh in her mind?

Somehow, two hours later, Mimi got the puppies settled and managed to make her meeting. After the meeting, she drove home, a woman in debt but an excited one. The space next to the coffee shop had been perfect; her cousin Rebecca had been ecstatic about Mimi's idea and planned to come the following week to start renovations. Mimi had spoken with the owner of the café, and he'd agreed to sell to her.

She would knock out the wall between his café—no, *her* café—and Rebecca's bookstore and combine the bookstore and coffee shop. They would have a special-events corner for entertainment. Mimi would offer storytelling and music programs for children, even some combination family/music programs for kids and adults, as well as offer the space to Seth for his support-group sessions where she could lead the cooking activities and maybe some art classes. Seth wouldn't even need his parents' funding. She slipped into the shower, wondering what Seth would think about her new business plan.

Plan. She actually had a career plan of her own now.

Pride warmed her, filled her with a giddiness that made her laugh. But a scraping sound jarred her. She paused and cut off the water, wrapped a bath towel around her and tiptoed to the bedroom. She peered through the window and shielded her eyes from the bright glare of the streetlight, then spotted an airplane flying precariously low, dragging some kind of sign, lit up like Christmas-tree lights. Probably one of her father's stunts.

She read the letters. Good heavens, the sign wasn't an advertisement for Wiley's used cars. The big flag was waving, "I love you, Mimi. Will you marry me?"

The faint sound of music drifted from below, then a howling. The wind. Another storm brewing? A cat maybe? A screech owl?

She scanned the ground and spotted Seth standing below the window, a portable CD player beside him. He was dressed in a black tux and held a guitar, strumming the chords off-key. A light snow had begun to fall, dotting his hair with white crystals. He looked handsome and sweet and so sexy her heart nearly burst.

The song he was trying to sing to her was one of her favorites. "'I love you, and you know I do.'"

Mimi stifled a giggle and propped her head on the windowsill. As he continued to butcher the song, the sincerity in the way he bellowed out the words tugged at her emotions.

"'I love you, and you know I do.'"

She stared into his eyes and realized that she did love him, loved him with all her heart, and that he loved her, too. Really loved *her.* The baby was a bonus.

Her earlier fears evaporated—just because her mother had left her didn't mean Seth would. She had to put him out of *their* misery and tell him how she felt.

"I love you, too, Seth. And yes, I'll marry you." She tossed the towel on the floor, smiling when his gaze found her naked body through the moonlit window. "Now, come here."

Seth dropped the guitar and stubbed his toe on the CD player as he raced up the porch to her. Seconds later he dragged her in his arms and sang the chorus again.

"'I love you, and you know I do.'" He threaded his hands in her hair and said in a husky voice, "I'll do anything for you, Mimi. If you want to pursue acting, we'll move to New York or California or wherever you want, and I'll support you."

She narrowed her eyes and brushed snow from his jacket.

"Emotionally, I mean, or what the hell, financially, too, if I want to. Marriage is a partnership. Sometimes you have to let the people who love you do things for you, 'cause you certainly do a lot for them."

"I do?"

"Yes, and if you want to work after the baby's born, I'll arrange my schedule to be home."

"Okay," Mimi whispered, tearing at his shirt. "I get the idea. But we're not moving anywhere." She quickly explained about turning down the job and the new venture she'd undertaken. "I'm going to call it Sugar Hill's Hotspot."

Seth's gaze softened. "Is that what you really want, Mimi?"

"Yes, I want to be your wife and a mother to our baby, and I want us to live here in Sugar Hill near our family—although we have to work on yours a bit, and we might need to change a few teensy-weensy things about the house."

Seth feathered kisses across her jaw. "Whatever you say. Whatever you want. We'll throw all the furniture away and start over." He belted into the chorus of the song again.

"Okay, okay," Mimi whispered with a giggle. "You can stop the serenade now."

Seth grinned wickedly. "I'm pretty bad, aren't I?"

Mimi laughed. "Yeah, but you're a fantastic lover. And you'll make a wonderful daddy."

He dipped his hand to tease her neck.

She said, her tone serious, "I'm sorry. I've been pretty difficult about stuff."

He nibbled at her neck and grinned. "Hormones."

"Sure, we can say that now, but what excuse will I have after the baby's born?"

Seth slipped his hand over her stomach. "I don't know. I might just have to keep you barefoot and pregnant."

"Sounds good to me," Mimi whispered. Except she did have a new business to run. He knelt and kissed his way down to her belly. Oh, well, she'd worry about that later. Much, much later.

Chapter Twenty

Seth stood in the middle of the gazebo on Mimi's grandmother's property on Pine Mountain, his knees knocking. Just his luck, his bride had insisted they write their own wedding vows. He'd pored over poetry books, listened to a litany of love songs on CD and even found a book on-line entitled *Love Letters,* but everything he'd read sounded too clichéd, too dramatic or too sappy.

He'd finally written a few words straight from his heart and scribbled them on the palm of his hand in case he got nervous and forgot—he'd just have to check his hand without letting Mimi see his little cheat sheet.

White chairs filled the lawn, the first spring bulbs peeked through the ground, and lilies and white-satin ribbons decorated the gazebo. His bride had been late today, sending him into a momentary panic and reminding him of his first near-wedding disaster, but she'd simply explained that her feet had swollen since she'd purchased her wedding shoes and she'd had to run out and buy a new pair. Sounded logical to him, at least Mimi's kind of logic.

A folk guitarist, Mimi's idea of course, strummed soft rock music, then moved into a more modern version of the "Wedding March." Grammy Rose waved a handkerchief at him and he grinned, remembering the last time he'd been here, the day she'd given Mimi her hope chest and he'd offered Mimi a ride— the day his life had changed and his whirlwind romance with Mimi had begun.

Hannah and Alison strolled down the center aisle, their tea-length pale-yellow dresses shimmering in the twilight, and took their places. Then Wiley appeared, decked out in a dark gray tux with a yellow ruffled shirt, and Mimi appeared beside him. His breath caught—she looked radiant in a snazzier, shorter rendition of a modern wedding dress with her wild hair piled on top of her head, curls spiraling out of a pair of silvery combs, lips painted a kiss-me red, hands clutching a bouquet of lilies.

Her smile set his insides on fire.

The preacher greeted them. "And who gives this woman in marriage?"

Wiley stepped forward and gestured toward Mrs. Hartwell, who was sitting on the front seat. "Her mother and I."

Seth took Mimi's slender hand in his and squeezed.

The preacher read a short scripture passage and commented on the sanctity of marriage. "I believe you've written your own vows?"

Mimi nodded enthusiastically. Seth's stomach

knotted. He angled his hand beside his jacket and flipped it over to read the first line, but the ink had disappeared. Panic hit him. His hand had been sweating so much he'd smeared the ink onto Mimi's hand!

"Seth?"

He saw Mimi looking at him expectantly. He'd have to wing it.

Seth Broadhurst had never winged anything in his life.

She was still staring at him, so he took a deep breath, gathered her hand in his and slowly slipped the golden band around her finger. "Years ago in college I heard an old folk song by John Prine. He sang a song about wanting a woman who could make a man's knees knock." He grinned at the stunned look on her face. "Mimi, you make my knees knock. You've given me laughter in my life, you've taught me how to have fun, but most of all you showed me how to love. You make my heart quiver with longing and my soul complete. I love you now and will love you forever and always."

Mimi wiped tears from her eyes and he winced, praying the ink didn't smudge onto her beautiful face. Then she noticed the ink stain and one eyebrow shot up. He mouthed the words *I love you,* deciding he'd probably use them daily to get him out of trouble with his wife.

Mimi shook her head slightly, indicating he was hopeless, then smiled, took his hand and slid a matching gold band on his finger. "Seth, you helped me find myself, you helped lead me to a peaceful place in my own soul so that I could love and be loved by another. You make me laugh, you make me dream, you make me want to grow old and share our stories with our grandchildren. I love you forever and always.''

Seth instinctively reached for her to draw her mouth to his, but the preacher cleared his throat. ''We'll get to that part in a minute, son.''

The guests laughed. ''Guess I'll forever be making a fool of myself over this woman,'' he said.

Mimi giggled and the crowd clapped.

''With the power now invested in me, I pronounce you husband and wife. *Now,* you may kiss the bride.''

Mimi blinked back tears at the love in Seth's eyes as he swooped her over his arm for a long, hungry kiss. Catcalls and whistles echoed behind them, then applause rang out. Even Seth's parents, who had surprised them by coming, smiled.

''I'm glad your parents changed their mind,'' Mimi said softly.

Seth nodded and lay a hand over Mimi's stomach in a protective gesture. ''I told them if they wanted any part of their grandchild's life, they had to accept us.''

Mimi nuzzled his neck as they started down the aisle. ''I say we cut the cake and get to the honeymoon fast.'' She hooked her arm through Seth's and headed toward the reception area, cutting a sideways glance at Alison. Her younger sister had brought a date, the ob-gyn who worked with Hannah. Would wedding bells be ringing for Alison next?

"I can't wait to throw the bouquet," Mimi whispered to Seth. "I have a feeling I know who will catch it."

Mimi saw Grammy's eyes twinkle. She wondered what Grammy would put in Alison's hope chest.

* * * * *

Don't miss youngest sister
Alison Hartwell's story in

HAVE HUSBAND, NEED HONEYMOON,

coming in July 2001, only from
Harlequin American Romance.

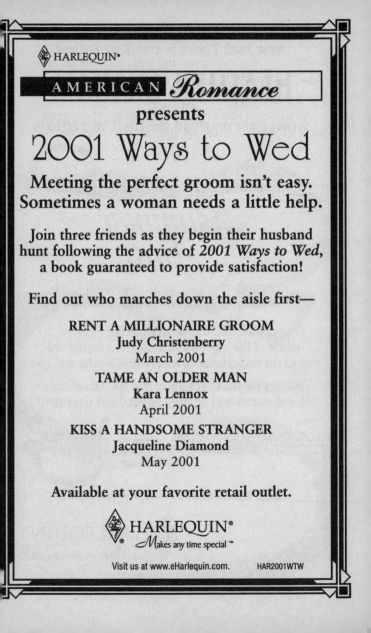